# RAVES FOR
# NICHOLAS MEYER . . .

"We may now fairly consider Meyer a legitimate heir to the mantle of Sir Arthur Conan Doyle . . . replete with covert love affairs, missing bodies, false clues, petulant suspects . . . THE WEST END HORROR is Sherlock Holmes and Dr. Watson at their finest."

—*St. Louis Post-Dispatch*

"I hope Nicholas Meyer never stops writing Sherlock Holmes pastiches because he does it so much better than anyone else . . . FANTASTIC ENTERTAINMENT."

—*The New Republic*

"More power to Meyer . . . the reader will breathlessly turn pages as the mystery swells to a bizarre climax . . . DEFINITELY A THREE-PIPE BOOK."

—*The Hartford Times*

"Meyer scores very high for invention, authenticity, and Sherlockian scholarship."

—*Boston Globe*

# . . . and THE WEST END HORROR . . .

# The West End Horror

*A Posthumous Memoir of*
*John H. Watson, M.D.*

as edited by

# Nicholas Meyer

BALLANTINE BOOKS • NEW YORK

A condensed version of *The West End Horror* originally
appeared in *Playboy* magazine.

Library of Congress Catalog Card Number: 75-38776

ISBN 0-345-25411-2-175

Manufactured in the United States of America

First Ballantine Books Edition: June 1977

*For Elly and Leonore*

# Contents

# Foreword

One of the interesting consequences of publishing *The Seven-Per-Cent Solution* has been the great number of letters I have received—in my capacity as editor—from all over the world. As I predicted at the time of publication, the manuscript has become the centre of a heated controversy, and people have written to me on all sorts of paper, with varying grammar, spelling, and punctuation, to tell me what they think about the book's authenticity. (I even number among my correspondents an eleventh grader in Juneau, Alaska, who called me on the phone quite early one morning—apparently supposing Los Angeles time to be an hour *later* instead of otherwise—to tell me that he thought I was a fraud.)

A more bizarre result of the book's appearance has been the surfacing of a number of other "missing" Watsonian manuscripts, to wit: no less than five, all submitted for my consideration as editor. They arrived from sources as diverse as their astonishing contents, from an airline pilot in Texarkana, Texas; a diplomat in the Argentine; a widow in Racine, Wisconsin; a rabbi in Switzerland (this one written in Italian!); and a retired gentleman of undefined occupation in San Clemente, California.

The manuscripts were all interesting, and all contained pedigrees, explaining their belated appearance and the circumstances under which they were composed. At least two of them—while perfectly charming—were obvious forgeries (one a pornographic put-on), a third a thinly disguised political tract, another the ravings of a disordered mind, the fourth attempt to prove Holmes's Jewish ancestry (this was *not* from the Swiss rabbi), and one . . .

The case you are about to read is taken from a manuscript that belongs to Mrs. C. K. Verner of Racine, Wisconsin. Before it was given to me, I received the following letter from Mrs. Verner, mailed to me, care of my publishers in New York:

December 14, 1974

Dear Mr. Meyer:

I was really interested to read the manuscript you edited, called *The Seven-Per-Cent Solution*. My late husband, Carl, was descended from the Vernet* family, which as you probably know, Sherlock Holmes was descended from, too.

I wonder if you would be interested in looking at another "long lost manuscript" of Dr. Watson's, only this one was never exactly lost. Carl, my husband, got it from his father, who was willed it (he used to tell us) from Mr. Holmes personally.

It is hand-written and a bit difficult to read in spots, mainly because of some water damage suf-

* Emile Jean Horace Vernet (1789-1863), called Horace Vernet, famous French painter and portraitist, was the great-uncle of Sherlock Holmes.

fered to it by Carl's father back in the 30s when he couldn't afford to fix the roof of his attic.

Carl's father (Grandpa Verner—he died in '46) never let any publisher see the manuscript because it's quite clear from the beginning of it that Mr. Holmes didn't want people to read it. But there's a lot of water under the bridge since then, and those people are all dead, anyway.

I read in the paper last week all about what they just found about Gladstone's personal life, and I guess this can't be any more hurtful than that.

Carl is gone since last February, and as you know, the economy is not doing too well. I'm probably going to have to sell the farm and could surely use some cash. If you want to see the papers and you are interested in them, we could come to some understanding about money. (I think I'll take your uncle Henry's advice, though, and try to sell the original copy! I think I read in *Time* magazine where he got a bundle on it from some jasper in New Mexico who collects stuff like that.)

Very truly yours,

Marjorie Verner (Mrs.)

This letter was the first of a great many which passed between Mrs. Verner and myself. On my advice, she consulted her family lawyer, and that individual proved (to my cost) to know his business. Eventually, however, matters were satisfactorily settled and I flew to Racine to pick up the manuscript after several Xeroxes had been made.

It was extremely difficult to read in places and presented very different problems from its predecessor's.

The water damage was severe. In places words and even phrases were obliterated and impossible to decipher. I was obliged to consult specialists in this sort of thing (and I give special thanks here to Jim Forrest and the laboratories at U.C.L.A.), who worked technical wonders at bringing up missing pieces.

There were many occasions, however, when the results were unsuccessful. Here I have been forced to put in the word or phrase that seemed to fit the rest of the paragraph or page. I have done my best, but I am not Watson, and thus the reader may find a jarring note here and there. For this he must blame not the good doctor but my humble self. I thought of indicating these passages in the book but then decided such bracketing would be too intrusive. I'm sure the worst offenses will be quite obvious, anyway, and my clumsy hand will be instantly perceived.

Aside from the water damage, the most nettlesome problem was dating the manuscript. Internal evidence makes it quite clear that *The West End Horror* begins March 1, 1895. Ascertaining the date of its composition, however, is another matter. It was evident (to me, anyhow) that it was composed a lot later than 1895. Not only does Watson refer to intervals of years between efforts on his part to get Holmes's permission for the project, he also points out that among considerations *pro* permission were the deaths of many of the principals concerned with the case. Inasmuch as these names are not changed (impossible to disguise really, as Holmes points out), the dates are fairly easily determined. They hint at a relatively late date of composition, certainly after 1905. The fact, however, that the manuscript is in Watson's own hand, indicates with equal clarity that he was not yet crippled by arthritis. Beyond that, it is difficult to say. My own hunch—and it is only a hunch—is that *The West*

*End Horror* was set down sometime after the First
World War and before Holmes's death, in 1929. One
of the things that makes me pick so late a period is
that Watson—as in *The Seven-Per-Cent Solution* (but
not so much)—continues to describe things that obviously aren't there any more. That Watson never sought
to recover the manuscript after Holmes's death suggests to me that his own ailments had begun to over-
take him (possibly the onslaught of crippling arthritis,
which plagued his last decade)—another argument for
the latish dating.

It may be noted that Watson's use of "Americanisms" persists, and this, I feel, deserves comment.
Readers skeptical of the authenticity of *The Seven-Per-
Cent Solution* base part of their argument for forgery
on the fact that the book contains these Americanisms,
which they deem "telltale." But they disregard two
very crucial points. In the first place, Americanisms
crop up all through Watson's case histories; in the
second, there is a very simple reason for this. Between
1883 and 1886, Watson was working as a physician
in San Francisco, California, to pay off some of his
brother's debts. He married his first wife, Constance
Adams, there, as any student of W. S. Baring-Gould's
excellent biography of Holmes and Watson * knows.
As Holmes (after living in America for two years) remarked to Watson, in *His Last Bow*, "My well of
English seems to be permanently defiled." So much
for Americanisms.

As for footnotes, I have again attempted to keep
them to a minimum, though there are so many facts
which check out (an argument in favor of the manuscript's authenticity) that I felt obliged to include
many of them.

* *Sherlock Holmes of Baker Street: A Life of the World's
First Consulting Detective*, by William S. Baring-Gould, published by Bramhall House, 1962.

Finally, a brief comment regarding the authenticity question. We have no way of proving such things. Indeed, healthy skepticism demands that we doubt. To have discovered one missing Watsonian account might seem like a miracle; to have unearthed another smacks suspiciously of coincidence. In self-defense I point out that I cannot claim to have actually discovered either of these documents, and in the case of the second, as Mrs. Verner points out, it wasn't exactly missing.

As regards authenticity, the reader must decide for himself, and I am aware of the controversy (am I ever!) that will surround this narrative. I conclude by referring you all to that charming poem of Vincent Starrett, which includes the wonderful words, "Only those things the heart believes are true."

Nicholas Meyer
Los Angeles
August 1975

# Introductory

"No, Watson, I'm afraid my answer must remain the same," said Sherlock Holmes. "You're setting down 'the West End Horror,'" he went on, chuckling at my expression. "Don't look so astonished, my dear fellow. Your thought process was simplicity itself. I saw you at your writing table, arranging your notes. Then you came upon something you had forgotten about; it stopped you cold; you held it, read it, shaking your head with an air of familiar disbelief. Then you turned your gaze to our collection of theatrical programmes and then to my little monograph on ancient English charters. Finally, you stole a surreptitious glance in my direction as I sat absorbed in tuning my fiddle. *Voilà*." He sighed and drew his bow across the strings in a tentative fashion, resting the end of the instrument on his knee. "I'm afraid it must still be 'No.'"

"But why?" I retorted with energy, not pausing to acknowledge his mental legerdemain. "Do you think I would fail to do justice to the case—or to yourself?" This last protest was tinged with irony, for his early criticisms of my efforts to keep some record of his

1

professional activities had been harsh, indeed. They had mellowed to something less than full approval when, with the passage of time, he saw that my accounts brought him more than a modicum of agreeable notoriety. His vanity, which was not inconsiderable, was usually flattered at the prospect.

"On the contrary. What I fear is that you *would* do justice to it."

"I shall change the names," I offered, beginning to see where the problem lay.

"That is precisely what you cannot do."

"I have done so before."

"But cannot possibly do so now. Think, Watson, think! Never have our clients been so well known! The public may argue about the true identity of the King of Bohemia *; they may guess at the real title of the Duke of Holderness. But here there could be no room for doubt—there are no fictitious characters you could substitute for those of the principals in this affair and hope to deceive your readers. To disguise them sufficiently, you would find yourself in phantasy up to the neck."

I confessed this difficulty had not occurred to me.

"Besides," Holmes went on, "you would be obliged to recount our part in the business, as well. While scarcely unethical, it could hardly be termed legal. Destruction of a corpse without notifying the authorities is a clear violation of law and could be construed in this case as suppression of evidence."

There the conversation ended—as it usually did—and I tucked away my notes on the entire incredible story till I should chance upon them again after

---

* Long assumed by scholars to be King Edward VII. However, Michael Harrison has recently demonstrated beyond a shadow of a doubt that the King of Bohemia was in reality His Serene Highness Prince Alexander ("Sandro") of Battenberg, once king of Bulgaria.

another year or two and broach the subject once more.

Getting Holmes to change his mind once he had got hold of an idea was like trying to reverse the direction of the global orbit. Once it had begun spinning on its course, it was virtually impossible to stem the momentum, let alone alter the axis. An idea would fix itself in his brain, take root there, and flourish like a tree. It could not be uprooted, only felled—and this only when struck by a better idea. It was Holmes's unshakable conviction in the present instance that "the West End Horror" (as he liked to call it) was a story for which the world was not yet prepared and that it could not be revealed save with consequences he wished to avoid.

Several things finally combined to change his views on the topic. The passage of years and the deaths of many of the principals involved, as well as the changing mores of society, wrought a subtle alteration in his obstinacy. Then I advanced a clever argument myself, which was designed to allay his fears of publication.

I told him in so many words that my chief concern was setting down the case as a matter of historical record (there he conceded its usefulness) and not as sensational literature for the scandalmongering Press. So far from looking for a publisher, I offered Holmes sole and exclusive proprietorship of the manuscript, to do with as he saw fit, *when* he saw fit. My only stipulation was that it not be destroyed.

He procrastinated for several days following my offer, during which he appeared to have forgot entirely our latest discussion (I think perhaps he was trying to) and busied himself with his criminal index, which demanded constant revision if it was to be of any use. I did not press him, knowing that his mind was turning over this new possibility without my having to say anything further.

"How could you possibly organise it?" he asked me once, while we were at the Turkish baths. "The cast of characters and events is large and diffuse. It will provide you with none of the compact symmetry of my more typical cases, the kind of material with which you work so well."

I answered that I should simply set down what happened in the order in which it happened.

"Oho," he laughed. "Resorting to the tricks of cheap fiction, are you? No one will believe you, you know."

I added that remark to my arsenal of incentives and aimed it back at him. He brooded over it amidst the rising steam and said nothing.

Another week went by, and then, quite abruptly, he looked up from his chaotic filing arrangements and said in an offhand tone, "Oh, well, you might as well do it. But see that you give it to me, as you promised, when you have done."

I did not dare say anything to provoke second thoughts on his part but replied with equal offhandedness that I would. And so I shall, making only one disclaimer before beginning. Since the case which follows involves a great many of the greatest names on the British stage, there is a great temptation to write the story today * with the benefit of that comforting hindsight, which allows us to claim with a certain smugness that we knew all along who was destined for greatness and other like matters. It may also strike the contemporary reader—should Holmes ever let this manuscript out of his hands!—that some of my suspicions at the time were nothing short of preposterous. I will resist the temptation to modify or dilute those

_____

* Another bit of evidence for the latish dating.

4

suspicions. I did not at the time, nor do I now, believe that positions of power or influence render a subject immune from investigation. My suspicions * may seem absurd today, but I will let them stand, for all that, and tell my story as it fell out at the time.

# ONE

# Sherlock Holmes in Residence

All theatrical London gossiped and speculated about the murder of Jonathan McCarthy when news of it first appeared in the papers. Theories were rife concerning the acerbic writer and the many enemies his pen had made. But curiosity, unsatisfied, eventually dies a death of boredom. McCarthy's assassin was never caught, much less discovered, and as no new facts were forthcoming, the police were finally forced to join the public and own themselves baffled. The case was never closed, but their interest was inevitably arrested by more current events. The mysterious death of the actress at the Savoy had the same tongues wagging for weeks, and Scotland Yard was hard put to explain the peculiar disappearance of its police surgeon—who vanished, taking two corpses along with him from the mortuary, and was never heard of again. In McCarthy's case the police ignored, as well (or forgot, because they could not understand it), the bizarre clue the dead man had left behind.

How the populace would have trembled had they deciphered it! Instead of being idly (or in the case of the police, professionally) interested in an affair which, however sensational, held no personal concern for them, they would have found themselves—all of them!—very real participants in a crime so monstrous that it threatened to blot the nineteenth century and alter the course of history.

The winter of '94–'95 had been a fearful one. Not in recent memory had London been pelted so with snow; not in recent memory had the wind howled in the streets and icicles formed on drainpipes and in the eaves as they did in January of 1895. The inclement weather continued unabated through February, keeping the street sweepers perpetually occupied and exhausted.

Holmes and I stayed comfortably indoors at Baker Street. No cases appeared out of the snowdrifts, for which we were unashamedly grateful. I spent much of the time organising my own notes after first extracting a promise from Holmes to desist from chemical experiments. I pointed out that in fair weather it was possible to dispel the stench he created with his test tubes and retorts by opening the windows and going out for a walk, but that should he become carried away now by his hobby we would inevitably freeze to death.

He grumbled a deal at this but saw the logic of it and settled down for a time to indoor target practise, one of his favourite recreations. For an hour at a time—as I sat at my desk and endeavoured to work—he reclined on the horsehair divan, his pistol propped between his knees, and squeezed off round after round at the wall above the deal table which contained his chemical apparatus.

He had managed to spell Disraeli with bullet pocks when this diversion, too, was denied him. Mrs. Hudson knocked at our door and told him in no uncertain terms that he was menacing the neighbourhood. There had been complaints from the house next door, she said, by an elderly invalid who claimed that Holmes's artillery was having a deleterious effect on her already unstable constitution. In addition, the reports had caused several large icicles to fall before they had melted sufficiently to be rendered harmless. One of these stalactites, it appeared, had nearly driven itself through the head of the dustman, who had threatened to bring an action against our landlady as a result.

"Really, Mr. Holmes, you'd think a grown man like yourself would be able to occupy his time in a more sensible fashion!" she exclaimed, her bosom heaving with emotion. "Look at all them fine books you have, just sittin' there, waiting to be read. And *there*—" she pointed to several bundles on the floor, tied with string— "some you haven't even opened as yet."

"Very well, Mrs. Hudson. You have carried the day. I will immerse myself." Holmes escorted her wearily to the door and returned with a disgruntled sigh. I was grateful that we no longer kept cocaine lying about, for in earlier times such frustrations and boredom would have provoked instant recourse to its dubious comforts.

Instead, Holmes took the landlady's advice and began cutting the strings on his parcels of books with a small penknife and inspecting their contents. He was a compulsive bibliophile, always buying volumes, having them sent 'round to our rooms, and never finding time to read them. Now he squatted down in their midst and began glancing at the titles of works he had forgot he owned.

"I say, Watson, look at this," he began, but subsided on to the floor with the tome in one hand whilst with the other absently felt into the pocket of his dressing gown for a pipe.

He devoured the book, along with several bowlsful

of shag (almost as malodorous as some of his chemicals), and then went on to another volume. He had become interested in ancient English charters and now prepared to devote himself to serious research on the subject. His preoccupation did not greatly astonish me, as I knew his range of interests to be wide, varied, and occasionally odd. He had mastered a number of arcane topics—matters quite unrelated to the art of criminal detection—and could speak brilliantly (when he chose) on such diverse matters as warships of the future, artificial irrigation, the motets of Lassus, and the mating habits of the South American jaguar.

Now English charters occupied his mind with a passion which totally conformed to his other pursuits in its single-minded application of his powerful intellect. He had apparently been interested in them at some earlier date, for most of the books he had purchased (and neglected to open) dealt with this peculiar subject, and at the end of the week the floor of our sitting room was virtually paved with them. Eventually such volumes as were at his immediate disposal were deemed insufficient for his purposes and he was obliged to sally forth into the snow and make his way to the British Museum for sustenance. These forays lasted for several afternoons during the last week of February, the nights which followed being spent in the laborious transcription of his notes.

It was a sunny, cold morning, March 1, when he flung his pen across the room in disgust.

"No use, Watson," said he. "I shall have to go to Cambridge if I am to approach this seriously. The material simply isn't here."

I remarked that his interest threatened to develop into a mania, but he appeared not to have heard me. He hunted up his pen on the floor whither he had hurled it and prepared to address himself again to his notes, observing the while, with a didactic formality which contrasted oddly with his posture upon hands and knees, "The mind is like a large field, Watson. It is available for cultivation only if the land is used sensibly and portions of it are permitted to lie fallow periodically. Part of my mind—my professional mind—is on holiday at the moment. During its leave of absence I am exercising another quarter of it."

"It's a pity your professional mind is out of town," I remarked, looking out of the window and into the street.

He followed my gaze from his position on the floor. "Why? What are you looking at?"

"I believe we are about to have a visitor, someone interested in that portion of your intellect that is currently lying fallow."

Outside, I could see stepping—or rather hopping nimbly—between the shovels of the snow cleaners and the brooms of the housemaids, one of the queerest creatures I had ever beheld.

"He certainly appears a likely candidate for admittance to 221b," I went on, hoping to distract my companion from the volumes which had failed him.

"I am not in the mood for visitors," Holmes returned moodily, thrusting his fists into the pockets of his dressing gown. "What does he look like?" The question was automatic and escaped his lips involuntarily.

"He isn't wearing a coat, for one thing. On a morning like this he must be mad."

"Clothes?"

"Norfolk jacket and knickerbockers—in this weather! They look well worn, even at this distance. He keeps adjusting his shirt cuffs."

"Probably false. Age?"

"Roughly forty, with an enormous beard, slightly

reddish, like his hair, which is blowing over his shoulder as he walks."

"Height?" Behind me I could hear a vesta being struck.

"Rather tall, I should say, under medium height."

"Gait?"

I pondered this, wondering how to describe the newcomer's hopping, skipping pace.

"The man walks like a gigantic leprechaun."

"What? Why, this sounds like Shaw." Holmes came up behind me, quite animated now, as we gazed together at the advancing figure. "Hello, it *is* Shaw. I'm blest if it isn't!" he exclaimed, smiling, his pipe clenched between his teeth. "Whatever brings *him* out on a morning like this? And what has made him change his mind and decide to pay me a visit?"

"Who is he?"

"A friend."

"Indeed?" No one as familiar as I with the personal life and habits of Sherlock Holmes could have received this statement with anything less than wonder. Aside from myself, his brother, and various professional acquaintances, I was not aware that Holmes cultivated any friends. The peculiar fellow advancing below us was now examining house numbers with some care before hopping on and stopping before our door. The bell rang with a truculent jingle several times.

"I met him at a concert of Sarasate's * some years ago," Holmes explained, turning to make some hasty order of our shambles. He kicked a few books out of the way, forging a path of sorts from the door to

---

* Sarasate was a well-known violin virtuoso of the day. For a full (though not entirely accurate) account of the meeting, see Baring-Gould's biography of Holmes.

a chair by the hearth. I seldom accompanied him any more to concerts and the opera, preferring more convivial amusements of the sort he found trivial.

"We got into a rather heated disagreement about Sarasate's abilities, as I recall, but finally buried the hatchet. He is a very brilliant Irishman." Holmes removed his pistol from the chair he proposed to offer our guest and put it on the mantel. "A brilliant Irishman who has not yet found his métier. But he will. He will. You will find him amusing, if naught else. He has got hold of some of the oddest notions."

"How do you know he is brilliant?"

We could hear a muffled conversation taking place at the foot of the stairs, doubtless between our visitor and Mrs. Hudson.

"How do I know? Why, he told me so himself. He has no qualms about hiding his light under a bushel. Furthermore," he looked up at me, the coal scuttle in his hands, "he understands Wagner. He understands him perfectly. This alone qualifies him for some magnificent destiny. At the moment, miserable man, he's as poor as a church mouse."

We could now hear feet rapidly ascending our stair.

"What does he do?"

There was a knock on our door of the same energetic variety which had manifested itself towards our bell some moments earlier.

"Oh, you want to be careful of him, Watson. You want to watch him and give him a wide berth." He added some coal to the fire and passed me with a conspiratorial finger on his lips as he went to the door. "He is a critic."

With this, he flung wide the door and admitted his friend. "Shaw, my dear fellow, welcome! Welcome! You have heard me speak of Dr. Watson, who shares

14

these lodgings with me? Ah, good. Watson, allow me to present 'Cornetti di Basso,' known to his intimates as Mr. Bernard Shaw." *

* Shaw wrote music criticism under the name Cornetti di Basso.

# TWO

# An Invitation to Investigate

Mr. Bernard Shaw's resemblance to an outsized leprechaun increased on closer inspection. His eyes were
the bluest I had ever beheld, the colour of the Côte
d'Azur. They twinkled with merriment when he spoke
lightly and flashed when he became animated, which
was not infrequently, for he was an emotional individual and a lively talker. His complexion was almost
as ruddy as his hair, and he boasted a disputatious
nose, broad and blunt at the tip, where the nostrils
twitched and flared. His speech added to the lepre-
chaunish impression he conveyed, for it was tinged
with the faintest and most pleasant of Irish brogues.

"By God, I believe your rooms are more untidy than
my own," he began, stepping across our threshold and
nodding to us both. "However, they are somewhat
larger than my hovel, which allows you to be creative
with your sloppiness."

I was annoyed by these remarks, which struck me
as an unseemly preamble for a guest, but he flashed
me an impish grin which managed, somehow, to take
away the sting of his words. Holmes, apparently used
to his brusque and forthright manner, appeared not
to have heard.

"You've no idea what a pleasant surprise this is," he informed the critic. "I'd quite given up hope of ever persuading you to set foot in these digs."

"I made a bargain with you," Shaw reminded him with some asperity. "I said that I would call upon you at your convenience if you in turn would attend a meeting of the Fabian Society." He accepted the chair indicated by Holmes and sat down, stretching forth his small hands and surprisingly skinny legs toward the comfort of our blaze.

"I'm afraid I must continue to decline your gracious invitation." The detective drew up a chair opposite. "I am not a joiner by nature, I fear, and while I would cheerfully dole out coin of the realm to hear you discourse on Wagner, you must permit me to go about the reformation of the race in my own way."

"You call it reformation?" the Irishman snorted. "Ha, you right wrongs, one by one, imagining yourself to be some sort of mediaeval knight errant." Holmes inclined his head slightly, but the other snorted again. "You are only addressing yourself to the effects of society's ills, not the causes, whereas the Fabians, with our motto, 'Educate, Agitate, Organise,' are trying to—"

Holmes laughed and held up a deprecating hand. "My dear Shaw, spare me your polemics at this hour of the morning. I trust, in any event, that you have not come to Mohammed on this frosty day to visit him with the philosophy of socialism."

"It wouldn't hurt you if I had," Shaw returned equably. "My eloquence on the subject has been declared alarming by those in a position to know."

"Even so. I can't offer you any breakfast—that's long since been cleared away—but in any case, I perceive by your right sleeve that you have already dined on eggs and—"

Shaw chuckled and inspected his sleeve. "That's

19

yesterday's breakfast. I see you are fallible. How comforting."

"Would you like some brandy? It will take the chill off your bones."

"And shorten my life by ten years," the elf replied with a merry smile. "Thank you, I'll remain as I am."

"You aren't prolonging your life by going about in this weather without a coat," I observed. He smiled thinly.

"I was obliged to pawn it yesterday, a temporary expedient until my next week's wages. A ludicrous state of affairs for a middle-aged man, don't you find? Critics are not revered as they should be."

"Shaw writes for the *Saturday Review*," Holmes informed me, "and apparently they pay no more for reviewing drama than the *Star* did for writing about music."

"Not by half," the Irishman agreed. "Could you manage on two guineas a week, Doctor? Your writing brings you a deal more, I daresay."

"Why don't you attempt something in a more lucrative vein?" I suggested. "You might try your hand at a novel."

"I've tried my hand at five and collected eight hundred rejections among them. No, I shall continue as critic and pamphleteer, occasionally turning out a play of my own on the side. Did either of you gentlemen happen to attend a performance of *Widowers' Houses* a year or two back?"

We shook our heads, I, for my part, never having heard of the play.

The Irishman did not appear surprised or put out. "It would have astonished me if you'd said yes," he remarked with mordant humour, "though it would have lent you a kind of distinction in the years to come. No matter, I shall keep at it. After all"—he held up his fingers—"all the great English playwrights are Irish. Look at Sheridan! Goldsmith! Look in our own time at Yeats, and look at Oscar Wilde! All Irish! One day Shaw will be included in that glorious pantheon."

The man's bumptiousness was past bearing.

"Shakespeare was English," I pointed out, mildly. Instantly I perceived I had struck an exposed nerve. Shaw paled, his beard quivered, and he leapt to his feet.

"Shakespeare?" He rolled the word around his mouth with scornful relish. "Shakespeare? A mountebank who had not the wit to invent his own plots, much less embellish them! Tolstoy was right—a conspiracy of nineteenth-century academia, that's what Shakespeare is. I ask you, do people really 'kiss away kingdoms,' or don't they rather hold on to power just as long and as tenaciously as they can? *Antony and Cleopatra*—what ineffable romantic twaddle! Claptrap! Humbug! They were as cynical a pair of politicians as you could conjure, both of 'em!"

"But the poetry," I protested.

"Poetry—rubbish!" His colour was changing again to a scarlet hue as he danced about the room, occasionally stumbling over the books on the floor. "People don't talk poetry, Doctor! Only in books—and bad plays! The man had a brilliant mind," he allowed, calming somewhat, "but he should never have wasted his intellect on plays. He should have been an essayist. He had not the gifts of a playwright."

This last statement was so completely astounding that I fancy Holmes and I must both have simply gaped at him for some moments—which he affected not to notice as he resumed his seat—before Holmes recovered himself with a little laugh.

"Surely you didn't come here this morning to take on Shakespeare any more than the evils of capitalism," said he, filling a pipe from the Persian slipper on the

21

mantel, "though I am tempted to dwell on the contrast between your views on the redistribution of wealth and your own desire for an increase in salary."

"You've swayed me from the point," Shaw acknowledged with a sour look, "with all this talk of Shakespeare. As for my salary, that you must take up with Mr. Harris, if you think you can face him. I have come to you this morning on quite a different errand." He paused, whether for dramatic effect or merely to collect himself, I could not tell. "There has been a murder done."

Silence filled the room. Holmes and I instinctively exchanged glances as Shaw surveyed us with evident satisfaction.

"Who has been murdered?" Holmes enquired calmly, crossing his legs, all attention now.

"A critic. You don't read the drama notices? Ah, well, then, you've missed him. Jonathan McCarthy writes for the *Morning Courant*—or wrote, I should say, since he will no more."

Holmes picked up a pile of papers by his chair. "I confine my attentions as a rule to the agony columns," he confessed, "but I can't have missed a story such as—"

"You won't find it in the papers—yet," Shaw interrupted. "Word of the deed was just circulating at the *Review* offices this morning. Instead of writing my piece due tomorrow, I came here straightway to tell you of it."

Throughout this recital, he attempted to maintain a jocular demeanour, as one who is not affected personally by such grisly tidings. Yet beneath his gallows-humour delivery, I sensed a very real anxiety. Perhaps the murder of a colleague threatened him in a way he could hardly have acknowledged.

"You came here straightway," Holmes echoed, filling his pipe with dextrous fingers. "With what end in view?"

The Irishman blinked in surprise.

"Surely that is obvious. I wish you to investigate the matter."

"Is it so very complicated? Will not the police suffice?"

"Come, come. We both know the police. I want neither their inefficiency nor a whitewash by the authorities. I want an honest, unbiased, and complete examination of the matter. I continue to read Dr. Watson's accounts of your doings in the *Strand* and long to see you in action for myself. Are you not up to the challenge? The man was stabbed," he added as incentive.

Holmes cast a longing look in the direction of his literary researchers, but it was clear he was interested, despite himself.

"Had he any enemies?"

Bernard Shaw laughed long and heartily.

"You ask that question about a critic? In any case, it must surely be obvious that he possessed at least one. For McCarthy I should postulate a score." He winked roguishly in my direction. "He was even less agreeable than I."

Sherlock Holmes considered this for some moments, then rose abruptly and threw off his dressing gown.

"Come, let us have a look. Have you the unfortunate man's address?"

"Number Twenty-four South Crescent, near Tavistock Square. One moment."

Holmes turned and regarded him.

"You are forgetting the matter of a fee."

"I haven't yet said that I will take the case."

"Nevertheless, I must tell you I am not capable of paying a brass farthing for your services."

"I have worked for less on occasion, if the matter

interested me." He smiled. "Are you still writing your treatise on Wagner?"

"*The Perfect Wagnerite,* yes."

"Then perhaps I shall trouble you for a signed first edition." Holmes slipped into his jacket and ulster. "*If* I take the case." He moved to the door, then stopped. "What is your real reason for wishing me to look into this business?"

The leprechaun threw out his hands. "The satisfaction of my own curiosity, I give you my word. If Dr. Watson pays his share of the rent with prose accounts of your work, perhaps I can do the same by putting you on the stage."

"Pray do not," Holmes responded, holding open the door for us. "I have little enough privacy as it is."

# THREE

# The Business at South Crescent

"Well, Watson, what do you make of him?" my companion demanded. We were sharing a hansom on our way to 24 South Crescent, where Shaw had promised to meet us. He had some business matters of his own to attend to in the mean time. I huddled into the recesses of my coat and pulled up my scarf against the biting wind before replying.

"Think of him? I must say I find him insufferable. Holmes, how can you tolerate the conversation of that know-all?"

"He reminds me of Alceste, I fancy. At any rate, he amuses me as much as Alceste. Don't you find him stimulating?"

"Stimulating?" I protested. "Come now, do you really suppose Shakespeare would have been better occupied writing essays?"

Holmes chuckled. "Well, admit I warned you that he held some queer ideas. With Shakespeare, unfortunately, you tumbled on to his *bête noire*. There, I confess, his views appear radically unsound, but then, his prejudices can be explained. He reads plays not as thou dost, Watson, but rather to take the measure of himself against the minds of other men. 'Such men

26

as he be never at heart's ease whilst they behold a
greater than themselves.'"

"'And therefore are they very dangerous,'" I concluded the passage for him. I looked out of the window
at snowbound London and found myself wondering if
the big leprechaun could be dangerous. Certainly, he
was handy enough with words to turn them into lethal
weapons, but there was something so impishly ingrati-
ating about the man that I found it hard to reconcile
my opinions of him.

"Here we are," my companion cried, interrupting
my reverie. We found ourselves in Bloomsbury, in a
pleasant, well-kept semicircle of houses which faced
private gardens maintained with equal devotion. The
area was at present covered with snow, but the out-
lines of a formal garden peeped through and affected
the contours of the drifts. The houses themselves were
four-storeyed and painted white. They were all boarding establishments, but I noticed no signs proclaiming
vacancies and decided the location was too desirable
and the charges probably too high for that. Number 24
occupied a space in the middle of the semicircle. It
looked no different from its neighbours to the left and
right, save for the crowd gathered before it and the
uniformed constables who barred the curious from
access to the open front door.

"I have a premonition we are about to meet an old
friend," Holmes murmured as we descended from the
cab. There was no great difficulty in our being admitted to number 24, as Holmes was well known to the
members of the force. They assumed he had been
summoned to view the situation in his capacity as consulting detective, and he did nothing to discourage
this belief as they passed us in.

The murdered man's flat occupied a first-floor suite
of rooms facing the gardens and was easily reached
at the top of the stairs. We hadn't opened the door

(which stood slightly ajar) before a familiar voice assailed our ears:

"Well, if it's not my old friends Mr. Holmes and Dr. Watson! What brings you gentlemen to South Crescent, as if I didn't know. Come in, come in!"

"Good morning to you, Inspector Lestrade. May we survey the damage?"

"How did you come to know there was any?" The lean, ferret-like little man shifted his gaze from one to the other of us. "It wasn't Gregson* sent you 'round, was it? I'll have to have a word with that cheeky—"

"I give you my word it was not," Holmes assured him smoothly. "I have my own sources, and they appear sufficient. May we have a look?"

"I don't mind if you do," was the lofty reply, "but you'd best be quick. Brownlow and his boys'll be here any minute now for the body."

"We shall try to stay out of your way," the detective rejoined and began a cursory examination of the flat from where he stood.

"The fact is, I was thinking of coming by your lodgings a bit later in the day," the Scotland Yarder confessed, watching him narrowly. "For a cup of tea," he added firmly, apparently for the benefit of a young, sandy-haired sergeant, who was the room's only other living occupant.

"Can't make head or tail of it, eh?" Holmes stepped into the room, shaking his head over the mess Lestrade and his men had made of the carpet. "Will they never learn?" I heard him mutter as he looked around.

The place combined the features of a library and sitting room. Lavishly equipped with books, it boasted

* Inspector Tobias Gregson, also of Scotland Yard. A perennial rivalry existed for many years between Gregson and Lestrade. On the whole, Holmes had a higher opinion of the former.

a small tea table, which at the moment supported two glasses containing what looked like brandy. One glass had been knocked on its side but not broken, and the amber liquid remained within it. Next to the same glass, a long, oddly-shaped cigar sat unmolested in a brass ashtray, where it had been allowed to go out of its own volition.

Behind the table was set a day bed and beyond that, facing the window, the writing table of the dead man. It was covered with papers, all related—so far as I was able to discern from a casual glance—to his calling. There were programmes, theatre tickets, notices of substitutions in casts, as well as cuttings from his own reviews, neatly arranged for easy reference. Beside these papers was an engraved invitation to the première of something called *The Grand Duke,* at the Savoy two days hence.

Those walls devoid of bookshelves were literally papered with portraits of various members of the theatrical profession. Some were photographs, others were executed in pen and ink, but all bore the signatures of the notables who had sat for them. One was assailed by the testimonials of affection from all quarters and awed by the likenesses of Forbes-Robertson, Marion and Ellen Terry, Beerbohm-Tree, and Henry Irving, who stared or scowled dramatically down at the visitor.

All these, however—the books, the desk, the pictures, and the table—were but as set decorations for the *pièce de théâtre.* The corpse of Jonathan McCarthy lay on its back at the base of a set of bookshelves, the eyes open and staring, the black-bearded jaw dropped, and the mouth wide in a terrible, silent scream. McCarthy's swarthy looks were not pleasant in and of themselves, but coupled with his expression in death, they combined to produce a truly horrible impression. I had seldom beheld a more unnerving sight. The man had been stabbed in the left side, somewhat below the heart, and had bled profusely. The instrument of his death was nowhere apparent. I knelt and examined the corpse, determining that the blood had dried on the silken waistcoat and on the oriental carpet beside it. The body was cold, and parts of it were already quite hard.

"The other rooms are undisturbed, I take it?" Holmes enquired behind me. "No handwriting on the walls?"

"Gad, sir, but you've a long memory." * Lestrade laughed. "No, the only writing on the walls is on those pictures. This room's where the business took place, all right."

"What are the facts?"

"He was found like this some two and a half hours ago. The girl came up with his breakfast, knocked on the door, and receiving no answer, made so bold as to enter. He'd overslept before, it seems, on more than one occasion. As to what happened, that's clear enough, up to a point. He was entertaining here last night—though he came home late and let himself in with his latchkey, so nobody got a look at his company. They sat down to a brandy and cigars here at the table when an altercation began. Whoever it was reached behind him to the writing desk and grabbed this." He paused and held out his hand. The young sergeant, taking his cue, passed over something wrapped in a handkerchief. Lestrade set it gently on the table and threw back the folds of material to reveal

---

* In 1881, the word *Rache* was found written in blood on the wall of an empty house in Lauriston Gardens. The only other feature of interest was the corpse of a man, recently murdered. Watson's account, titled "A Study in Scarlet," was the first of Holmes's cases to be written up. It was published in the Beeton's Christmas annual of 1887 under the pen name of Watson's literary agent, Dr. A. Conan Doyle.

an ivory letter opener, its yellowish blade tinged a tawny red, some of which had run onto and splattered the finely worked silver hilt.

"Javanese," Holmes murmured, examining it with his magnifying glass. "It came from the desk, you say? Ah, yes, here is the sheath which matches it. Go on, pray."

"Whoever it was," Lestrade resumed with a self-important air, "seized the letter opener and stabbed his host, knocking over his brandy glass as he thrust home. McCarthy crumpled in a heap at the foot of the table while the other departed, leaving his cigar burning where he had left it. McCarthy stayed beneath the table for some time—you can see quite a pool of blood—and then with his last reserves of strength, he crawled to those bookshelves—"

"So much, as you say, is obvious," Holmes observed, drily, pointing to a ghastly scarlet trail which led directly to the body. He stepped forward and carefully picked up the cigar, holding it gently in the middle. "This cigar is less so. I cannot recall having ever seen one like it. Can you, Lestrade?"

"You're going to tell me about all those tobacco ashes you can recognise," the inspector scoffed.

"On the contrary, I am trying to tell you about one I cannot. May I have a portion of this?" He held up the cigar.

"As you wish."

Holmes inclined his head in a little bow of thanks. He withdrew his penknife, leaned on the edge of the table, and carefully sawed off two inches of the cigar, putting the stub back where he had found it and pocketing the sample where it would not be crushed. He straightened up ready with another question, when a noise was heard below, followed by a thunderous rush upon the stairs. Shaw arrived, breathless but triumphant.

"Why, man," he cried, "your name's a regular passe-partout! Well, where's the carrion?"

"And who might this gentleman be?" Lestrade growled, looking fearlessly up into Shaw's beard.

"It's all right, Inspector Lestrade. He's a colleague of the deceased, Mr. Bernard Shaw of the *Saturday Review*." The two men bowed slightly.

"There's a police wagon arrived downstairs with a stretcher in it," Shaw informed Lestrade.

"Very good. Well, gentlemen, as you can see——"

"You haven't yet told him about the book, Inspector," interposed the young sergeant shyly. He had been following Holmes's every move with eager interest, almost as though trying to memorise his actions.

"I was going to, I was going to!" Lestrade shot back, growing more annoyed by the minute. "You just stay in the background, young man. Pay attention and you'll learn something."

"Yes, sir. Sorry, sir."

His chief grunted. "Now where was I?"

"You were about to show us the book poor McCarthy had used his last ounce of energy to retrieve," Holmes prompted quietly.

"Oh, yes." The little man made to fetch the volume, then turned. "Stop a bit. Here, how did you come to know he was after a book before he died?"

"What other reason for him to have struggled so valiantly towards the bookshelves," Holmes replied mildly. "A volume of Shakespeare, is it not? I perceive one is missing."

Instinctively I stole a glance at Shaw, who heard this information with a snort and began his own examination of the room.

"Kindly refrain from trampling the clues," Holmes ordered sharply and signed for him to join us by the table. "May we see the book?"

Lestrade nodded to the sergeant, who brought forth

another object, wrapped in a second handkerchief, which he placed on the table. Before us lay a volume of *Romeo and Juliet* published by Oxford and obviously part of the complete edition which rested on the shelf above the corpse. Holmes brought forth his glass again and conducted a careful examination of the volume, pursing his lips in concentration.

"With your permission, sir." It was the sergeant, again.

"Yes?"

"When we found it, it was opened."

"Indeed?" Holmes shot a keen glance at Lestrade, who shifted his weight uncomfortably. "And where was that?"

"The book wasn't in his hands," the little man replied defensively. "He'd let go of it when he died."

"But it was open."

"Ay."

"To what page?"

"Somewheres in the middle," Lestrade grumbled. "It's a perfectly ordinary book," he added testily. "No secret messages stuck in the binding, if you're thinking along those lines."

"I am not thinking at all," Holmes replied coldly. "I am observing, as you, evidently, have failed to do."

"It was page forty-two," the sergeant volunteered. Holmes favored him with an interested look, then began carefully turning the bloodstained pages.

"You're very keen," he commented, studying the leaves. "How long have you been down from Leeds? Five years?"

"Six, sir. After my father—" The sergeant stopped short in confusion and regarded the detective with amazement.

"Here, Holmes," his superior broke in, "if you know the lad, why not say so?"

"It is no great matter to infer his birthplace, Les-

trade. Surely you can't have failed to remark on his
distinctive *a*'s and his peculiar manner of handling
diphthongs? I would hazard Leeds or possibly Hull,
but then, he has been in London these last six years,
as he says, and acquired a local overlay, which makes
it difficult to be precise. You live in Stepney now, don't
you, Sergeant?"

"Ay, sir." The sergeant's eyes were wide with awe.
For his part, Shaw had listened to the entire exchange
with the strictest attention stamped on his features.

"But this is wonderful!" he shouted. "Do you mean
you can actually place a man by his speech?"

"If it's in English, within twenty miles.* I'd know
your Dublin origins despite your attempts to conceal
them," Holmes answered. "Ah, here we are, page
forty-two. It concludes Act three, Scene one—"

"The duel between Tybalt and Mercutio," Shaw
informed Lestrade, who was still pondering, I could
see, the detective's linguistic feat. Holmes looked at
him sharply over the volume, whereat the Irishman
coloured slightly.

"Well, of course I've read it," he snarled. "Romantic twaddle," he added, to no-one in particular.

"Yes, the death of Mercutio—and also Tybalt.
Hmm, a curious reference."

"If he made it," Lestrade persisted. "The book
wasn't in his hand, as I've said, and the pages might
have fallen over in the interim."

"They might," Holmes agreed. "But since there is
no message in the book, we must infer that he meant
to tell us something with the volume. It could hardly

---

* In 1912 Shaw wrote *Pygmalion,* a play very obviously
inspired by Holmes, about an eccentric bachelor with the same
gift for placing people by their speech. Dr. Watson finds his
counterpart in Colonel Pickering, who like Watson, has met
his roommate on his return from Indian climes.

have been the man's whim to pass the time with a little Shakespeare while he bled to death."

"Hardly," Shaw agreed. "Even McCarthy would not have been capable of such a gesture."

"You don't seem very disturbed by what's happened to the deceased," Lestrade observed suspiciously.

"I'm not disturbed in the slightest. Except by his browsing Shakespeare at the last. The man was a charlatan and a viper and probably merited his end."

"Shakespeare?" Lestrade was now totally perplexed.

"McCarthy." Shaw pointed at the photographs and sketches. "You see those signatures on the walls? Lies, every one of 'em. I'll swear to it. Proffered in fear."

"Fear of what?"

"Bad notices, malicious gossip, scandal in print or out of it. McCarthy kept his ear to the ground. He was notorious for it. Do you remember the suicide some three years ago of Alice Mackenzie? She played the lead in that thing by Herbert Parker at the Allegro*? Well, that was almost certainly provoked by an item with this blackguard's name on it."

Sherlock Holmes was not listening. As we watched, he proceeded to give the room a thorough inspection of the kind only he could manage. He crawled about on all fours, peering through his glass; he examined the walls, the shelves, the desk, the table, the day bed, and finally made the most minute inspection of the corpse itself. Throughout this tour, which lasted some ten minutes or more, he kept up a running commentary of whistles, exclamations, and mutterings. Part of this time was spent in examination of the other rooms in the flat, though it was clear from his expression when he returned that Lestrade had been accurate

---

* This is fiction on Watson's part or Shaw's. I can find no mention of a scandal involving such a theater, author, or actress. There may have been such a tragedy, of course, but if there was, the names have been changed.

in saying that the drama had not overflowed the confines of the library.

At length he straightened up with a sigh. "You really must learn not to disturb the evidence," he informed Lestrade. He turned to the young sergeant. "What is your name?"

"Stanley Hopkins, sir."

"Well, Hopkins, in my opinion, you'll go far,* but you oughtn't to have touched the book. It might have made all the difference in the world had I been able to see the relation between the man's fingertips and the volume. Do you understand?"

"Yes, sir. I shall see that such a thing never happens again. We neither of us touched the body," he added in a gallant attempt to redeem himself in the detective's eyes.

"Good lad. Well, gentlemen, I think that is about all."

"And what have you uncovered with all your creeping and crawling about that I haven't?" Lestrade demanded with a sour grin.

"Nothing very much, I grant you. The murderer is a man. He is right-handed, has a working knowledge of anatomy, and is very powerful, though somewhat under six feet—as calculated by the length of his stride. He wore new boots, expensive and probably purchased in the Strand, and he smoked what is definitely a foreign-made cigar, purchased abroad. And before he left, he tore out the page in McCarthy's engagement diary with his name on it. Good day, Inspector Lestrade."

---

* Holmes's prediction proved correct. Hopkins became chief inspector in 1904 and had a forensic laboratory named for him upon his retirement in 1925.

# FOUR

# Concerning Bunthorne

On our way downstairs, we passed the police surgeon, Mr. Brownlow, and his men with the stretcher. Holmes exchanged a few words with that grey-bearded individual, with whom he had a nodding acquaintance. We then passed through the police barriers outside, and Holmes withdrew his watch.

"I'm in the mood for lunch," he declared, sucking in the cold fresh air and looking about. "Watson, this used to be your stamping ground; where shall we dine?"

"There's the Holborn; it's not far from here."

"Excellent. Let us repair to it for sustenance. Are you coming, Shaw?" He began to walk through the dirty snow at a smart pace, obliging the critic to skip briskly.

"How can you even think of food after what you have just witnessed?" Shaw cried in dismay.

"It is because of what I have witnessed that I find it crossing my mind," the detective returned. "Food is one of the principal means by which death is avoided."

"I really ought to be at work," Shaw growled as he sat down with us at the Holborn and eyed askance the Masonic tiling with which the establishment was

38

decorated. "I've two pieces due by noon tomorrow, and I haven't begun either of 'em yet." In spite of which statement he showed no disposition to leave.

"Watson," Holmes turned to me, his face hidden by the menu, "what do you say to some Windsor soup, beefsteak pie, roly-poly pudding, and a respectable Bordeaux?"

"That would suit me down to the ground."

"Good. Shaw, my dear fellow?"

"Certainly not. I am no carnivore, preying upon my fellow creatures. You may order me a small salad."

Holmes shrugged and gave our order to the waiter. It nettled me, I confess, to have my eating and drinking habits constantly challenged and rebuked by this waggish fellow. Furthermore, I perceived that far from paying Holmes for his services, the Irishman was now prepared to accept his luncheon as part of the detective's largesse.

We sat in silence for some moments, awaiting our meal and listening to the hubbub around us: the chat of the many customers crowding the restaurant at midday, the clatter of cutlery, and the incessant swinging of the doors that led to the kitchen. Holmes paid no attention to the chaos, but sat lost in thought, his eyes closed and his chin sunk upon his breast. With his great hawk's bill of a nose, he resembled nothing so much as some sleeping bird of prey.

"Well?" Shaw demanded, tiring of watching him. "Will you take the case?"

Holmes did not move or open his eyes. "Yes."

"Excellent!" The Irishman beamed, his countenance wreathed in smiles. "What must we do first?"

"We must eat." Holmes opened his eyes in search of our waiter, who arrived at that moment, carrying a large tray. Suiting action to the word, the detective refused to utter so much as a syllable for the next thirty minutes. He cheerfully ignored all Shaw's insistent enquiries but favoured that peppery individual with a smile every now and then by way of encouragement.

More familiar with his humours than was the critic, I did my best to contain my speculations and addressed myself to my own victuals, until at length Holmes took a final sip of wine, patted his mouth delicately with his napkin and proceeded to fill his pipe.

"You're not going to smoke!" Shaw protested. "Great heavens, man, are you intent on killing yourself?"

"The case is not without its features of interest," my companion began as though the other had not spoken. "Young Hopkins has a career unless I am very much mistaken. Are there any points which occur to you, Watson?"

"Aside from the business of the book, I must confess I was perplexed by the manner in which rigor mortis had set in," I replied. "One does not expect to find it so pronounced in the neck and abdomen and so conspicuously absent in the fingers and joints."

"Hmm."

"But what about the book?" Shaw interposed, excitedly. "Surely its importance cannot be overestimated. It must have been a ghastly ordeal for him to reach it."

"I do not underestimate its importance, I assure you. I merely question its value at the moment. Oh, I have encountered such evidence before." He waved a languid hand. "In a man's dying extremity, he tries to communicate the name of his murderer or else that murderer's motive. Unfortunately, without knowing more of Jonathan McCarthy than any of us do at present, it is highly unlikely that his *outré* clue can be forced into yielding much of value. What are we supposed to infer from it? That he saw himself as Mercutio? As Tybalt? That he was involved in a familial vendetta? Is it a word, a phrase, a passage, or a character that we are looking for? You see?" he threw out both hands in an expressive gesture. "It tells us nothing."

"But he must have thought otherwise," I protested.

"He must indeed. Or possibly he could not think of anything else in the crisis. I doubt he could have managed pen and paper, even had he reached them—and they were farther away, still. Then again, the clue may be perfectly obvious to a specific individual for whom he intended it." He shrugged.

"Then where do we begin?" Shaw demanded, puzzled. He was brushing his beard forward with his fingers into rather a fierce attitude.

Holmes smiled.

"Dunhill's would seem as likely a point of departure as any."

"Dunhill's?"

"They may be able to assist me in identifying the origins of the murderer's cigar. I shall go there after luncheon. In the meantime, I suppose we might begin with Bunthorne. Any idea who that might be?"

"Bunthorne?" We stared at him, I, for one, never having heard the name. He smiled yet more broadly, then drew forth his pocket book and produced a torn piece of paper from it.

"This is from McCarthy's engagement diary."

"I thought you said his murderer had pinched his engagements for February the twenty-eighth."

"So he did. This, as you can see, is for February the twenty-seventh, and I pinched it."

"It contains but one entry," I observed, "for six-thirty at the Café Royal."

"Precisely. With someone named Bunthorne."

Shaw silently reached forward and took up the paper, a scowl on his face, rendering his features more comical than usual. Abruptly he broke into an amused chuckle of appreciation.

"I can tell you who Bunthorne is—and so could anyone else in the West End, I fancy, but as you don't frequent anything but Covent Garden and the Albert Hall, I doubt very much if you'd know."

"Is he famous, then, this Bunthorne?" I asked.

The critic laughed again. "Quite famous. One might even say infamous—but not under that name. My late colleague appears to have noted his engagements in a sort of code."

"How do you know for whom Bunthorne stands? Is it a nickname?" Holmes enquired.

"Not precisely. Still I daresay he would answer to it." Shaw spread the paper out and jabbed at it with a thin forefinger. "It's the restaurant that makes it certain. He is usually to be found there, holding court."

"Holding court?" I ejaculated. "Who the devil is he, the Prince of Wales?"

"He is Oscar Wilde."

"The playwright?"

"The genius?"

"What links him with this 'Bunthorne'?" Holmes wondered.

Shaw laughed once more. "For that you must be familiar—as I suspect you are not—with the comic operas of Messrs. Gilbert and Sullivan. Do you never go to the Savoy?"

"*The Mikado* and so forth?" Holmes shook his head and relit his pipe.

"Then you are missing the greatest combination of words and music since Aristophanes, Wagner excepted. Bunthorne is to be found in *Patience*."

"I have heard the tunes, I expect, on the barrel organ."

"Of course you have. Every hurdy-gurdy in London grinds all Sullivan's music interchangeably." He regarded Holmes with a trace of scorn. "On what planet do you spend your time?" he wondered. "You are at least familiar with 'Onward Christian Soldiers' and 'The Lost Chord'?" He was amazed, I could see, by the detective's ignorance, which nonetheless did not seem strange to me. Sherlock Holmes was the man who once said it was a matter of utmost indifference to him whether the earth circled the sun or the sun the earth, provided the fact did not affect his work. Aside from his own particular musical interests (which leaned towards violin concerts and the grand opera), nothing was less likely than his knowing anything of London's fads and rages. He ignored Shaw's gibes and persisted with his own line of enquiry.

"Tell me about *Patience*," he demanded.

"Just a moment," I cried, rubbing my forehead. "It comes to me now. Holmes, when I returned from Afghanistan in eighty-one, I saw this play! At the Savoy, was it?" I turned to Shaw.

"I believe it opened the theatre," the critic assented.

"I'm almost certain of it, though I can't remember what it was about, for the life of me. I always forget the plots and so forth within a week or two. I remember this one because I couldn't understand what it was about at the time I was watching it—soldiers and someone with very long hair who was liked by all the chorus."

"Can you be more precise?" Holmes asked Shaw.

"The opera parodies the whole Oscar Wilde cult of aestheticism in rather a smart fashion. It was lost on you, Doctor, because you were out of the country when Wilde and his cronies burst upon the scene. Wilde himself appears in the piece in the person of Reginald Bunthorne—'A Fleshly Poet.'" Shaw grinned, coughed, and broke into song, his voice proving to be surprisingly musical, a pleasant, not quite robust baritone that caused a nearby head or two to turn in our direction:

If you're anxious for to shine in the high aesthetic
line as a man of culture rare,
You must get up all the germs of the transcendental
terms, and plant them everywhere.

You must lie upon the daisies and discourse in
novel phrases of your complicated state of mind,
The meaning doesn't matter if it's only idle chatter
of a transcendental kind.

And every one will say,
As you walk your mystic way,

"If this young man expresses himself in terms too
deep for *me*,

Why what a very singularly deep young man this
deep young man must be!"

Seeing that we made no move to interrupt, he went
on:

Then a sentimental passion of a vegetable fashion
must excite your languid spleen,
An attachment *à la* Plato for a bashful young potato,
or a not too French French-bean!

Though the Philistines may jostle you will rank
as an apostle in the high aesthetic band,
If you walk down Piccadilly with a poppy or a lily
in your mediaeval hand.

And every one will say—

Here he broke off, coughing again and looking
embarrassed.

"It goes something like that for another verse or so. Anyhow, that's Bunthorne—and depend upon it, that's Oscar." He looked at his watch. "Heavens, I must be off. I've had my fun, and now I must pay for it. Where shall we meet? I want you to catch me up on what progress you make."

"Willis's for supper?" I hazarded.

"That's a trifle rich for my blood."

"What about Simpson's?"

"Very well." He started to rise. "A little before eight?"

"One moment." Holmes laid a hand on his arm. "You know Mr. Wilde personally?"

"I know him, though not well. We are too awed by one another's gifts, with the result that we intimidate ourselves."

Holmes maintained his loose hold on the critic's arm. "Is he really a genius?"

"Oscar? Some of the cleverest people in London suppose so—Harris, Max Beerbohm, Whistler—"

"Do you?"

"What does it matter whether he is or is not a genius and if I think so or not?"

"I am trying to understand the dramatis personae in this business. You didn't think much of Jonathan McCarthy; I should like your estimate of Oscar Wilde."

"Very well," he frowned, gnawing a bit of his beard. "Yes. I would say definitely yes, he is a genius. His plays will be remembered as among the most scintillating in the language—and they are the least of his creations. *Patience*, on the other hand, will become passé within his lifetime.* A genius," he repeated,

---

* Shaw's ability to predict the future popularity of plays and operettas is questionable. He postulated an early demise for Sardou's play, *Tosca*, which in operatic form enjoys the same robust health as *Patience*.

unwillingly, "but he is courting ruin."

"Why?"

Shaw sighed and considered how best to answer the question. It was more difficult than I would have imagined for him to frame a response.

"I am not at liberty to be specific," he temporized after a pause.

"Then be general," Holmes advised.

Shaw thought again, his Mephistophelian brows arching in concentration. "Oscar has antagonised the world," he began, choosing his words with care. "He delights in antagonising the world. He doesn't take it seriously." He put his hands on the table and interlaced the fingers. "But the world does. The world takes it very seriously and is not inclined to forgive him for it. The world is waiting to take vengeance. There are sacred rites and conventions which will not be flouted."

"Mr. Gilbert has flouted them for years, hasn't he?" I asked. "Are they howling for his blood, as well? I don't believe it."

Shaw looked at me. "Mr. Gilbert's private life is beyond reproach. Or if it isn't, Mr. Gilbert is discreet. The same cannot be said of Oscar Wilde." He rose abruptly, as though annoyed with himself for having spoken too much. "Good day, gentlemen."

"Shaw," Holmes looked up languidly. "Where can we find Wilde?"

"These days I believe he puts up at the Avondale, in Piccadilly. Good day," he said again and bobbed his head in elfish acknowledgement before leaving with that curious dancing gait.

Sherlock Holmes turned to me. "Coffee, Watson?"

We proceeded after lunch to Dunhill's, in Regent Street, where Mr. Fitzgerald, who knew the detective well, examined the bit of cigar we exhibited.

"Dinna tell me you're at a loss," the Scot laughed, his blue eyes twinkling as he took the cigar.

Holmes was not amused. "I can identify twenty-three kinds of tobacco from the ash alone," he responded somewhat testily, it seemed to me. "When you have told me what this is, I shall have incorporated a twenty-fourth into my repertoire."

"Ay, ay," the honest fellow went on chuckling as he bent over the thing. "Well, it's foreign but not imported by anyone I know," he began.

"So much I had already deduced."

"Did you, indeed? Ay, well that narrows the field." He held it up and smelled it. "From the scent and the wrapping, I'd say it was Indian." He turned it back and forth between his thumb and forefinger, holding it to his ear and listening to the crackle, then sighted along its length like a rifle. "A cheroot. Notice the square-cut end and the heavy proportion of Latakia? They're a great favorite with the boys in the Indian army, but then those laddies'll smoke anything. I doubt I'd have the stomach for it, but I've heard you can acquire a taste for them."

"You can't buy them in England?"

"No, Mr. Holmes, I don't believe you can. They're too tough for civilians, as I've said, though some of the lads come home with boxes because they know there're none to be found here."

"Mr. Fitzgerald, I thank you."

"Not at all, Mr. Holmes. Does it figure in a case?"

"It may, Mr. Fitzgerald. It may."

# FIVE

# The Lord of Life

Holmes and I had of course seen caricatures of Oscar Wilde. Over the years his strange haircut, corpulent physique, and outlandish mode of dress had become familiar to us—as to all—through countless pen-and-ink sketches in various papers. And though we had not seen either play, we were aware that the brilliant Irishman was the author of two comedies playing simultaneously to packed houses. His latest, *The Importance of Being Earnest,* had opened only a fortnight or so before and been highly endorsed by the critics and public alike.

Yet neither the cartoons nor the articles by or about the man nor yet his plays themselves (had we seen them) could have prepared us in the slightest for the living embodiment of Oscar Wilde.

After our stop at Dunhill's we trudged 'round to Piccadilly and presented ourselves at the Avondale, enquiring after the playwright.

"You'll find him in the lounge," the clerk informed us with a dour expression.

"I take it that is from whence all this noise emanates?" asked Holmes politely. The man grunted by way of reply and busied himself behind the counter.

There was certainly a great deal of noise coming from the direction of the lounge, and Holmes and I followed it to its source, frankly curious. The clinking of glasses and the babble of animated, overlapping voices were discerned, the latter punctuated by sudden, shrill bursts and hoots of laughter.

My first impression, upon entering the room, was that I had journeyed backwards in Mr. Wells's time machine and stumbled upon a Roman Saturnalia of some sort, peopled by satyrs, Pan-like cherubs, and elves. A second glance assured me that the dozen or so young men gathered there, singing, reciting poetry, and drinking each other's health, were all dressed in the garb of the present century, albeit some of it rather askew. It took but a moment to realise who was chiefly responsible for this Attic impression. Standing in the centre of the room and towering over his guests both in size and stature was the leviathan Oscar Wilde himself. His odd long hair was wreathed with laurel or something very like it, and his deep, rich, and sonorous voice dominated the place as much as did his person.

Oblivious of the pandemonium, he was declaiming a poem having to do with Daphnis and Chloe (I was able to catch only a snatch here and there through the confusion of sound), with his arm draped over the shoulders of a slender young man whose blond curls framed the face of an angel.

After a moment or two our presence on the threshold made itself felt, and one by one all the revellers subsided, their songs and jests dying on their lips— save only Wilde himself. With his back to the door, he continued unaware of the intrusion, until the gradual halt in merriment caused him to turn and face us. One disagreeably flabby hand reached up and tugged the vine leaves from his tangled dark hair. His face was astonishingly comely and youthful, though I knew he must be forty. Too much food and too much drink had taken their toll and bloated his features. Nevertheless, his eyes were grey and clear and alert, his expression pleasing. Only his thick, sensual lips and his girth told of the dissipations in which he indulged.

As he focussed his gaze upon us, subdued whispers circulated, speculating about our business. More than once I caught the word *policemen*.

"Policemen?" Wilde echoed. His voice was soft as a caress and deep as a monastery bell. "Policemen?" He came forward slowly, carrying his coronet, and inspected us attentively. "No, no," he concluded with a ravishing smile. "I think not. By no means. There is nothing so unaesthetic on the planet as a policeman."

This provoked a few titters in the background. I noticed that when he spoke he had the odd trick of covering his mouth with a crooked finger. He looked at Holmes with interest, and the detective returned his gaze with a steadfast regard of his own. Their grey eyes locked.

"We may be less aesthetic than you think," Holmes told him without blinking, and reaching into his breast pocket, he presented his card. The urban Dionysus took in its contents with a careless glance.

"Dear me, dear me," he murmured without surprise. "*More* detectives. Not a very aesthetic lot, you force me to agree. I shall not dissemble, however, and pretend I haven't heard of Mr. Sherlock Holmes." The subdued revellers passed the name around behind him in reverential tones, a lone giggle marring the seriousness of the response. "And this must be Dr. Watson," Wilde went on, swivelling his luminous eyes in my direction and taking inventory. "Yes, it must; it positively must. Well," he sighed and collected himself with his charming smile, "what is it you gentlemen wish? Can I offer you some refreshment?"

"A minute or two of your time in private, sir, no more."

"Is it about the Marquess?" he demanded, his voice rising and beginning to tremble. "If so, I must tell you the whole affair is now in the hands of my solicitor, Mr. Humphreys, and you must take the matter up with him."

"It is about Jonathan McCarthy."

The playwright's dreamy eyes bulged briefly. "McCarthy? Then he has dared, after all—" his thick lips compressed with a show of annoyance coupled with resolve.

"He has dared nothing, Mr. Wilde. Jonathan McCarthy lies dead in his flat this day, the victim of a fatal assault by a person or persons unknown—some hours after his rendezvous with you at the Café Royal. I really think this interview might better be conducted elsewhere," Holmes concluded in a low tone.

"Murdered?" It took Bacchus a moment or two to grasp the meaning of the word. In that instant I perceived the truth of Shaw's observation. Wilde might antagonise people and defy convention, but he didn't really mean it or understand it to be harmful. Underneath his carefully nurtured decadence and his depraved, perverse ideas, the man was an utter innocent, far more shocked by the idea of murder than I was—and I fancied myself a deal more conventional than he.

"Come this way," he offered, composing himself, and on unsteady legs led us into the adjacent writing room. There was one elderly gentleman there, but his hat was over his eyes, his legs stretched before him, and it was clear that what the revelry next door had failed to accomplish, we need not even try. Holmes and I took seats, and Wilde threw himself heavily on to a sofa opposite. He made none of his public pretences to grace, but sat with his fat hands dangling between his knees, like a cabby's on the box, wearily holding a pair of non-existent reins.

"I take it I am under suspicion in the matter?" he began.

"Dr. Watson and I do not represent the police. Where their suspicions may fall, we have no way of knowing, though I may say from past experience"— Holmes smiled—"they occasionally take some quaint directions. Can you account for your whereabouts after your meeting with Jonathan McCarthy?"

"Account for them?"

"It may be helpful—for the police—should you be able to furnish them with an alibi," I pointed out.

"An alibi, I see." He leaned back with something like a smile. I caught another glimpse of him then, and I was reminded of Cassius's "aweary of the world." Despite an essentially humourous and sunny disposition, the man laboured under some terrible burden.

"Yes, that's all right," he brightened now without conviction, "I was with solicitor Humphreys. Tell me, how was it managed?"

"I beg your pardon?"

"The murder, my dear fellow, the murder!" His eyes gleamed as he warmed to the topic. "Was there incense burning? Did you find the footprints of a naked woman who had danced in his blood?"

Ignoring his macabre associations, Holmes briefly outlined the circumstances of the critic's death, omitting the business with the book and adding instead his own observation that no-one we had spoken with thus far appeared either surprised or grieved by the news.

Wilde shrugged. "I can't imagine the West End will consider him a great loss, no."

"What was the nature of your appointment with him yesterday?"

"Must I tell you?"

"We have no means to coerce testimony," Holmes

answered, "but the police are another matter. At the moment they do not know of your appointment."

Wilde's eyes flashed with hope in an instant, and he sat up straight in his chair.

"Is that true?" he cried clasping his hands. "Is that really true?" Holmes assured him that it was. "Then all may yet be well!" He looked from one to the other of us, his elation subsiding as he realised we must still be dealt with. "Better you than the police, is that it?" he sighed. "How life sometimes resembles Sardou, don't you find? What a pity! For Sardou." He chuckled at his own wit and ran a chubby set of fingers through his unruly hair.

"Was your meeting connected with your visit to a solicitor this morning?" Holmes prompted.

"In a way, I suppose you might think so. You gentlemen did not know Jonathan McCarthy, did you? No, I can see you didn't. How can I explain to you what that man was?" He rubbed his lips meditatively with the crooked forefinger. "Have you heard ever of Charles Augustus Milverton?"

"The society blackmailer? Our paths have not yet crossed, but I know of him." *

"That simplifies matters. Jonathan McCarthy pursued a similar line of country."

"He was engaged in blackmail?"

"Up to the neck, my dear Holmes, up to the very neck. He did not prey upon society, as Milverton does, but rather upon us denizens of the theatre. He had his sources, his little spies, and he squeezed hard. Of course the world of the theatre overlaps the social world now and again. At all events, I've had some experience of blackmailers and know how they must be dealt with. They get hold of letters I've written

---

* Holmes's path crossed Milverton's right before the latter's murder in January 1899.

from time to time and threaten me with them. But I
have a cure for that."

I asked him what that might be, and he smiled behind the crooked finger.

"I publish them."

"Was McCarthy threatening you with a letter?"
Holmes asked.

"With several. He'd heard about the business at the
Albemarle* earlier in the day and sent me an earnest
of his intentions."

"You will have to speak more plainly, I'm afraid."

Wilde sat back, pale, astonishment writ large upon
his features.

"But you've heard! Surely you've heard! It must be
across all of London by now!"

"Everywhere but Baker Street," Holmes assured
him drily.

Wilde licked his purplish thick lips and eyed us
nervously. "The Marquess of Queensberry," he began
in a voice hoarse with emotion, "the father of that
splendid young man back there in the lounge—but no
more like him than Hyperion's like Hercules—left a
card for me at the Albemarle, yesterday. I do not
propose to tell you the words the barbarian wrote on
that card—beside the fact that he misspelled them
—only that having read the words, I was not prepared
to ignore them.† I was advised by several friends to
do so, but I did not. I went 'round to Mr. Humphreys
after dinner (he was referred to me by my friend Mr.
Ross), and this morning he accompanied me to Bow
Street, where I swore out a complaint for criminal
libel. By this time tomorrow, the Marquess of Queens-

---

* Wilde's club.
† Written on the card by Queensberry: "To Oscar Wilde
posing as somdomite." Watson must have known the contents
of this notorious message when he set down the case but tactfully omitted them.

berry will have been arrested and charged, and soon I shall be rid for ever of that monster in human clothing. Hence the little celebration next door," he concluded with a sheepish grin.

"And McCarthy, you say, heard of the incident at the Albemarle?"

Wilde nodded.

"I believe he knew of Queensberry's intentions beforehand. He notified me and arranged a meeting at the Café Royal, where he declared his willingness to furnish certain correspondence of mine to the Marquess and his solicitors. He felt these documents would certainly prejudice my case."

"And were you of that opinion?"

"It was not necessary yesterday, nor is it necessary today that I answer that question. I had cards of my own to play, and I played them."

"I think it may be as well to lay them on the table now."

"As you like. To be brief, I am the repository of a great many secrets myself, concerning alarums and excursions in the West End. Theatre people are so colorful, don't you find? I know, for example, that George Grossmith, who does the patter songs for Gilbert (he played me, you know!), has been taking drugs. Gilbert scares him so at rehearsals that he has had recourse to them. I know that Bram Stoker keeps a flat in Soho, the existence of which neither his wife nor Henry Irving is aware. I cannot explain to what use he puts it, but my intuition tells me it isn't to play chess. Then again, I know about Sullivan's games of chemin de fer with—"

"And what did you know of Jonathan McCarthy?" Holmes interrupted, concealing his distaste.

Wilde replied without hesitation, "He was keeping a mistress. Her name is Jessie Rutland, and she is an ingenue at the Savoy. For a man who played the part of middle-class British rectitude to hypocritical perfection, such a disclosure would mean instant ruin. He understood that at once," Wilde added as an afterthought, "and very shortly we discovered that we had nothing to say to one another. A sordid story, I fear, but mine own."

Holmes stared at him for some moments, his face devoid of expression. He rose abruptly, and I followed suit.

"Thank you for your time, Mr. Wilde," said he. "You are certainly a font of information."

The poet looked up at him. There was something so ingenuous and pleasant in his countenance that I found myself charmed despite everything he had said.

"We are all of us as God made us, Mr. Holmes— and many of us much worse."

"Is that yours?" I enquired.

"No, Doctor—" he smiled slightly—"but it will be." He turned again and faced the detective. "You do not approve of me, I fear."

"Not altogether."

Wilde would not relinquish his eyes. "I find myself wishing that you did."

"It may be that one day I shall."

# SIX

# The Second
# Murder

It was twilight when Holmes and I left the Avondale and joined the rush-hour crowds in Piccadilly. The wind had risen, and it cut our faces, biting our throats, too, as we walked. Cabs were not to be had for love or money, but the Savoy Theatre was no great distance from the hotel. We simply trudged in that direction, elbowing our way amidst the throng and avoiding as best we could the dirty piles of snow shoveled up next to the kerbs.

I remarked as we walked that I could not remember encountering a more singular set of people than those we had met in connection with the murder of Jonathan McCarthy.

"The theatre is a singular calling," Holmes concurred. "A noble art but a dreary profession and one that reveres that which the rest of society condemns." He favoured me with a sidelong glance. "Deception. The ability to dissemble and deceive, to pass for what you are not. You will find it better expressed in Plato. These, however, are the actor's stock in trade."

"And the stock in trade of those who write their speeches for them," I noted in addition.

"You will find that in Plato, as well."

We walked for a time in silence.

"The chief difficulty with this case," he observed at length, as we entered the Strand, "besides the fact that our client cannot afford to pay for his meals, let alone our expenses—the chief difficulty, I say, is the super-fluity of motives. Jonathan McCarthy was not a well-liked individual, that much seems clear, which only serves to complicate matters. If half the tales Wilde told us just now are true, there may be upwards of a dozen people whose interests would be well served by eliminating him. And they all dwell within that cir-cumscribed world of the theatre, where passions—real and feigned—abound."

"What is more," I pointed out, "their professional gifts are likely to render their complicity in a crime rather more difficult than usual to detect."

Holmes said nothing, and we walked in silence a few paces more.

"Has it occurred to you," I went on, "that Mc-Carthy's use of Shakespeare was meant to be taken generally?"

"I don't follow you."

"Well, your friend Shaw—our client—cannot abide Shakespeare. The *Morning Courant,* for which Mc-Carthy wrote, is well known as a rival to the *Saturday Review.* There can be little doubt that with McCarthy out of the way, Bernard Shaw's star and literary fol-lowing would rise more or less together. Could Mc-Carthy's reference to *Romeo and Juliet* possibly mean not the Montagues and Capulets but rather the two periodicals? Doesn't Mercutio, dying, refer to 'a plague *on both your houses*'?" I continued, warming to my theme. "At the same time, the use of Shake-speare, whom Shaw detests, might serve to point an unerring finger in his direction as the assassin."

"Watson, what a devious mind you possess!" Holmes stopped, his eyes twinkling. "That is positively brilliant. Brilliant! Of course, you have neglected all the evidence, but I cannot fault your imagination." He resumed his steps. "No, I'm afraid it won't do. Can you honestly envision our Shaw drinking brandy? Or smoking a cigar? Or running his rival through—apparently on impulse—with a letter opener?"

"He's almost the right height," I contended feebly, not wishing to abandon my theory without a struggle. "Besides, his objections to drink and smoke might merely have been lodged for our benefit."

"They might," he agreed, "though I have known of his prejudices in those directions for some time. In any event, why would he come to me at all if he wished to remain undetected?"

"Perhaps his vanity was flattered by the prospect of deceiving you."

He considered this briefly in silence.

"No, Watson, no. It is clever but rather too cumbersome, and what is more, his footwear does not match the impressions left by the assassin. Shaw's shoes are quite old—it pains me to think of his walking about with them in this weather—whereas our man wore new boots, purchased, as I think I said, in the Strand. Oscar Wilde, at least, was wearing the right shoes."

"What of Wilde, then? Did you notice that when he spoke, he continually covered his mouth with his finger? Do you accept at face value his story of having checkmated McCarthy's blackmail scheme with knowledge of the man's illicit liaison?"

"I neither accept it nor reject it at the moment," he returned, undaunted. "That is why we are at the Savoy. As for Wilde's peculiar habit of covering his mouth, you surely observed that his teeth are ugly. It is merely improbable vanity on his part to conceal them in conversation."

"Did you see his teeth?"

"Didn't I just say he makes a considerable effort to hide them?"

"Then how do you know they are ugly?"

"Elementary, my dear fellow. He does not open his mouth when he smiles. Hmm, the house is dark, to-night. Let us go 'round by the stage door and see if there are folk within."

We walked into the alley that led to the stage door and found the door open. There was activity within the theatre, though it was clear from the bustle back-stage that no play was in progress. We threaded our way amongst actors and stagehands until our presence was discovered by the manager, who politely enquired as to our business there. Holmes tendered his card and explained that we were in search of either Mr. Gilbert or Sir Arthur Sullivan.

"Sir Arthur ain't here, and Mr. Gilbert's leading the rehearsal," we were told. "Perhaps you'd best speak with Mr. D'Oyly Carte. He's in the stalls. Right through this door and very quiet, gentlemen, please."

We thanked the man and stepped into the empty auditorium. The house lights were on and I marvelled once again at the lighting in the Savoy. It was the first theatre in the world to be totally lit by electricity, and the resultant illumination differed greatly from that supplied by gas. I thought back fifteen years and tried to recall my first visit to the place. I had worried then about the danger of fire originating from an electrical failure, since I could not understand who Reginald Bunthorne was supposed to be and allowed my mind to wander from the piece. My fears were apparently without foundation, because years have gone by since and the Savoy still stands unharmed.

A lone figure was seated in the stalls towards the back, and he favoured us with a baleful stare as we walked up the aisle in his direction. He was a small man, dwarfed by his chair, wearing a dark, pointed beard that complemented his black eyes. Something in his glower, at once so regal and so forbidding, made me think of Napoleon. It was my subsequent impression that this was his intention.

"Mr. Richard D'Oyly Carte?" Holmes asked when we were close enough to be heard in a whisper.

"What do you want? The press is not permitted here before opening nights; that is a rule at the Savoy. There's a rehearsal in progress, and I must ask you to leave."

"We are not from the papers. I am Sherlock Holmes, and this is my associate, Dr. Watson."

"Sherlock Holmes!" The name had produced the desired effect, and D'Oyly Carte's countenance broke into a smile. He half-rose from his chair and proffered two seats beside him. "Sit down, gentlemen, sit down! The Savoy is honoured. Please make yourselves comfortable. They have been at it all day and are at rather low ebb just now, but you are welcome, nonetheless."

He appeared to think we had entered his theatre on a whim, having for some reason taken it into our heads to attend a rehearsal. For the present Holmes encouraged this view.

"What is the name of the piece?" he enquired in a polite undertone, slipping into his seat beside the impresario.

*"The Grand Duke."*

We turned our attention to the stage, where a tall man in his late fifties, of military bearing, was addressing the actors. I say "addressing them," but it would be more truthful to say he was drilling them. It seemed in no wise inconsistent with his military stamp, which marked him as a compulsive man of precision. The stage was devoid of scenery, making it difficult to understand what the piece was about. Gilbert—obviously the military fellow was he—directed a tall, gangling actor to repeat his entrance and first speech. The man disappeared into the wings only to emerge seconds later with his lines, but Gilbert cut him off in mid-sentence and requested him to do it again. Next to us our host made several rapid notations in a book propped upon his knees. With some little hesitation the actor retreated once more upon his errand. Though nothing was said, it was clear that all were fatigued and that tempers were fraying. Carte looked up at the stage, pen in hand, a scowl creasing his features. He tapped the stylus nervously against his teeth.

"They're played out," he proclaimed in a mutter directed to no one in particular. From his inflection, it was impossible to determine whether he meant the players or the authors.

The actor made his entrance a third time and launched into his speech, getting somewhat further along before the author interrupted and asked him to repeat it.

"Our visit here is not entirely a social one," Holmes leaned towards the impresario. "I believe there is a young woman attached to the company by the name of Jessie Rutland? Which is she?"

The manager's demeanour underwent an instant metamorphosis. The harassed but generous impresario became the suspicious property owner.

"Why d'ye want to know?" he demanded. "Is she in any difficulty?"

"The difficulty is none of hers," Holmes assured him, "but she must respond to some questions."

"Must?"

"Either to me or the police, quite possibly to both."

Carte regarded him fixedly for a moment, then slumped into his seat, almost willing it to swallow him.

"I could ask for nothing more," he mused darkly. "A scandal. There has never been a breath of scandal at the Savoy. The conduct of the members of this company is beyond reproach. Mr. Gilbert sees to that."

"Mr. Grossmith uses drugs, does he not?"

Carte stared at him from the recesses of his chair, wonder written on his face.

"Where did you hear such a thing?"

"No matter where, the story will go no further than it has. May we speak with Miss Rutland now?" Holmes pursued.

"She's in her dressing room," the other replied gruffly. "Not feeling well—said something about a sore throat."

On stage voices were being raised. "How many times will you have it, Mr. Gilbert?" the actor exploded.

"Until I have it right will do, Mr. Passmore."

"But I've done it fifteen times!" the actor wailed. "I'm not Mr. Grossmith, you know. I am a singer, not an actor."

"Both facts are evident," Gilbert responded coldly. "However, we must do the best we can."

"I will not be spoken to in this way!" Passmore declared, and shaking with anger, he stamped into the wings. Gilbert watched him go, then turned his attention to the ground, apparently studying something there.

Carte rose to his feet. "Gilbert, my dear, let's halt for supper."

The author gave no sign of having heard.

"Ladies and gentlemen—" Carte raised his voice and adopted a cheerful timbre—"let us forbear for two hours and renew our energies over supper. We open within thirty-six hours, and we must all sustain our strength. Played out," he muttered again as the group on the stage started to disperse.

"The dressing rooms are downstairs?" Holmes asked as we got to our feet.

"Women stage left, men stage right." The impresario waved us absently towards the proscenium, absorbed by a more immediate crisis. We had started down the way we had come when the air was rent with an unearthly wail. So odd was the noise that for a moment no-one was able to identify it. In the empty theatre the hideous sound echoed and reverberated. The people on stage, preparing to leave, stood momentarily frozen with surprise and collective horror.

"That's a woman!" Holmes cried. "Come on, Watson!" He dashed across the footlights and into the wings, his coattails flying as I followed. Backstage, we plunged into a labyrinthine mass of theatrical apparatus that obstructed our path to the wrought iron spiral steps which led to the dressing rooms below. Behind us we could hear the pounding feet of the chorus, hurrying in our wake.

At the foot of the steps a passage led off to our left, and Holmes flew down it. A series of doors on either side of the corridors, some of them ajar, led to the ladies' dressing quarters. Holmes flung these open in rapid succession, stopping abruptly at the fifth door and blocking my view with his back.

"Keep them out, Watson," said he quietly and closed the door behind him.

Within seconds a group of thirty or so members of the Savoy company surrounded me, all babbling questions. I was struck with the ironic observation that they sounded like themselves—that is to say, like a chorus of Savoyards, singing, "Now what is this and what is that and why does father leave his rest, at such a time of night as this, so very incompletely dressed?" Suddenly into their midst, parting them firmly left and right as though he were breasting the Red Sea, strode Gilbert. His muttonchop whiskers bristled, his blue eyes were very bright.

"What is happening here?"

"Sherlock Holmes is endeavouring to find out," I

gestured behind me to the closed door. The large blue eyes blinked in the direction of the door, then refocussed themselves on me.

"Holmes? The detective?"

"That is correct. I am Dr. Watson. I sometimes assist Mr. Holmes. The woman who screamed, I take it, was Miss Rutland," I went on. "She complained of not feeling well, and you sent her downstairs to rest."

"I dimly remember doing something of the kind." He passed a weary hand over his broad forehead. "It has been a tiring day."

"Do you know Miss Rutland well, sir?"

He answered my question automatically, too preoccupied to object to my forwardness in quizzing him. "Know her? Not really. She is in the chorus, and I do not engage the chorus." A trace of bitterness crept into his voice, undisguised. "Sir Arthur engages the singers. Sir Arthur is not here at the moment, as you have quite possibly divined. Sir Arthur is either at cards with some of his titled friends or else at the Lyceum, where he is wasting his talents on incidental music for Irving's new *Macbeth*. It would be too much to ask him for the overture to our piece before opening night, but I daresay he will deign to have it ready by then. Perhaps Sir Arthur will even find time to coach the singers once or twice before we open, but I am not sure." Now he turned and spoke to the company. "Here, everybody!" he cried, "go and have your supper. We shall continue at eight o'clock sharp with Act One from the sausage-roll number. Go on and eat, my dears; there's nothing of consequence that need detain you here, and you must keep up your strength!"

They dispersed on cue, Gilbert patting a head occasionally or saying something encouraging in a low voice to another as they passed by, until we were alone. For all his military gruffness, a reciprocal bond of affection and trust between him and the players was evident.

"Now let me pass," he ordered in a tone that brooked no objection. Before I could answer, we were interrupted by a clatter on the spiral stairs at the end of the corridor as Carte descended hurriedly with another man, whose black bag proclaimed him a member of the same profession as myself.

Carte, rushing towards us, cried, "Dr. Watson, this is Dr. Benjamin Eccles, the doctor who is on call at the Savoy." I shook hands briefly with a man of medium height and pale complexion, with deep-set green eyes and a small, delicate-looking nose.

"I make the rounds of several theatres in the district when I am on call," Eccles explained, looking past me at the closed door, "and I'd just stepped into the stalls to see how the rehearsal was getting on when Mr. Carte saw me and summoned me downstairs, as he seemed to think I might be needed." He glanced from one to the other of us—uncertainly, confused, perhaps, by the presence of another physician.

Behind us the door opened and Holmes stood there in his shirt-sleeves. Clearly he had only been waiting for the members of the chorus to depart. I introduced Dr. Eccles, and Holmes favoured him with a curt inclination of his head.

"There has been a murder," he announced in sombre tones, "and all must remain as it is until viewed by the authorities. Watson, you and Dr. Eccles may come in. Mr. Gilbert and Mr. Carte, I must ask that you remain beyond the threshold. It isn't a pretty sight," he added under his breath, standing aside to let me in.

The sight, indeed, had little to commend it. A young woman with dark russet hair, who could not have been more than twenty-five, lay on her side upon a small sofa, which constituted the sole article of furniture in the room, save for a dressing table and chair. Her nap had been rudely interrupted by a crimson gash across her pearl white throat, and her life's blood, quite literally like a leaky tap, dripped on to the floor, where it had begun to collect in a small pool.

The sight was so horrible, the corruption of her existence so woefully and inappropriately complete, that it robbed us of articulation. Eccles coughed once and set about examining the wretched creature's remains.

"Her throat has been severed quite cleanly," he reported in a faint voice. "It is slightly hard above the cut. Can rigor have set in so quickly?" he asked himself. "It isn't present in her fingers, and her blood is still—is still—"

"She complained of a sore throat," I explained, suppressing an hysterical impulse to giggle at the thought. "Her glands are merely swollen." As I said this, it occurred to me that my own throat felt raw— a ghastly enough identification.

"Ah, that must be it." Eccles looked about the small room. "I don't see a weapon."

"It is not here," Holmes replied. "Or if it is, my search has failed to reveal it."

"But why, *why*? Why was she slain?" Carte shouted from the doorway, his small hands clawing clumsily at his collar and tearing it asunder. "Who would want to do such a thing?"

No-one was able to answer him. I looked at Gilbert. He had sunk on to a bench across from the entrance to the room and was staring glazily before him.

"I didn't know her at all well," he spoke woodenly, like one in a dream. "Yet she always seemed sweet enough and willing. A sweet young thing," he repeated, his eyes beginning to blink rapidly.

"There is nothing further for us here, Watson," Holmes declared, resuming his jacket and ulster.

Carte rushed forward and seized him by the lapels. "You can't go!" he cried. "You mustn't! You know what this is about! I insist that you tell me. What questions were you going to put to the girl?"

"My questions were for her ears alone," the detective replied solemnly. Gently he removed the other's quaking hands. "You may refer the police to Dr. Watson and myself for our depositions. They know where we are to be found. Come, Doctor." He turned to me. "We have an appointment at Simpson's which now assumes greater importance."

We bowed and shook hands with Gilbert, who responded in a trance, leaving Carte and the shaken Dr. Eccles, who would write up the relevant particulars of his examination. Poor man, he was more used to sore throats than cut ones, I fancy.

As we walked down the corridor, I heard Carte suggest to Gilbert that the rest of the rehearsal be cancelled.

"We can't," Gilbert replied in a hoarse rejoinder, his voice cracking with emotion.

# SEVEN

# Assaulted

Simpson's Café Divan was but a few yards farther along the Strand, and it was no great matter to get there from the theatre.* Nevertheless, as we left the Savoy and stepped on to the pavement, the frigid wind hit me like a wave and I stumbled against the kiosk next to the ticket office.

"Are you all right, Watson?"

"I think so—only a bit dizzy."

Holmes nodded sympathetically. "It was quite warm inside—and appalling. I confess to feeling slightly faint myself." He took my arm, and we entered the restaurant.

At this hour Simpson's was by no means full. We were recognised at once by Mr. Crathie and experienced no difficulty in obtaining a table. It wanted fifteen minutes of eight, granting us some moments for private reflection regarding the unexpected turn events had taken. I, for one, did not feel in the least like eating. I was aware, however, of an overpowering thirst and ordered a brandy and a carafe of water. The

---

* It still isn't. Simpson's and the Savoy remain happily extant, though both have been since rebuilt.

brandy burned along my throat like fire, and I found I could not swallow enough water.

"If we persist in tramping about in this weather," Holmes noted, "we are bound to catch our death." He, too, drank a good deal of water and looked, I thought, paler than was his wont.

We sat for some moments, studying our menus without enthusiasm, each wrapped in his own thoughts. Around us the restaurant was filling with animated diners.

"The case begins to assume a familiar shape," Holmes stated, setting aside the wine list.

"Which shape is that? I am utterly at a loss, I confess."

"A triangle, if I am not mistaken. I shall be greatly astonished if it does not prove to be the old story of a jealous lover, discarded by his mistress in favour of another patron. Possibly a more powerful one," he added darkly. He reached into his jacket and withdrew his pocketbook, carefully extracting again the slip of paper from Jonathan McCarthy's engagement calendar.

"It must be a very peculiar triangle," I countered, "if it includes so odd an angle as McCarthy. Are you asking me to believe that sweet-faced young woman took up with a man of his stamp? My mind rejects the whole idea."

"I must ask your mind to remain open a little longer, Doctor, for she *did* take up with him. At least, the evidence points strongly in that direction."

"What evidence?" My head had begun to throb almost as badly as the old wound in my leg.

"Wilde's, of course. If his information about George Grossmith's recourse to drugs elicited the response it did from Carte, we may, I think, grant its accuracy— at least provisionally—in other areas, as well. What have you to offer in rebuttal of such a charge? Her innocent appearance and the testimony of Gilbert, who by his own admission scarcely knew her. The latter information rebuts itself. As for the former," he mused, staring dreamily at the paper before him, "what can a woman's appearance signify? Women are devious creatures, even the best of them, and capable of vastly more than we men would like to suppose. That she was McCarthy's mistress, I am prepared to credit on the basis of the evidence so far; what her motives were for so being, I am prepared to learn."

"From whom?"

He shrugged. "I fancy that will depend to a degree on Arthur Sullivan. He hired her; it is to him I shall turn for a better portrait. Hullo!" He sat forward suddenly, pulled forth his magnifying glass, and held it over the torn scrap, scrutinising it beneath the lens.

"What is it?"

"Last night's entry, or I am much mistaken. Have a look." He moved the paper over to where I could see and held the glass above it for my benefit. Enlarged beneath the lens I saw faint impressions, evidently formed by a pencil pressing down on another piece of paper.

"There is something there!" I exclaimed.

"I think so, too, though whether it will be of any use to us is problematical." He looked about and hailed a nearby waiter, importuning him for a pencil. When the man had delivered it and gone, Holmes threw back a corner of the white tablecloth and positioned the paper carefully upon the wood. Holding the pencil at the mildest possible angle, he began to rub the lead lightly back and forth across the surface of the sheet. Slowly, like a spirit photograph, the indentations appeared in sharp relief:

Jack Point—here

"Who can that be?" we wondered simultaneously.

"Here is our oracle in these matters," Holmes observed, looking up. "Perhaps he can help us."

Shaw stood at the entrance to the restaurant, still without a coat (it caused my teeth to chatter just to look at him). He held his nose in the air as though sniffing the place out, unwilling to put a foot forward until certain of his welcome. Holmes held up a hand and waved him over. He advanced rapidly and slid on to the banquette without ceremony as the detective replaced the tablecloth and deftly slid the paper back into his pocketbook.

"What have you learned?" the critic demanded without preamble. "I'm famished," he volunteered before either of us could answer and began a perusal of the menu.

"We wish to consult you first," Holmes said easily. "Do you know of anyone named Jack Point?"

Shaw looked up from the menu, knitting his brows.

"Jack Point?" he repeated cautiously. "No, I can't say that I do. Why?"

"Could it be someone in the theatre world? An actor perhaps?" Holmes persisted. The critic's frown of puzzlement deepened.

"Or the name of another Gilbertian creation?" I struck in.

He brightened at once, snapping his fingers.

"Of course. *Yeomen of the Guard!* Another of their operas," he explained. "A serious one, laid in the Middle Ages and having to do with the Tower of London."

"And Point? Who is he?"

"A jester—rather a foolish and pathetic figure; he loses his lady love to a highborn lord, if my memory serves."

Holmes smiled sadly. "Ah. Jack Point is our man, no doubt. You see, Watson? We are dealing with that geometrical construction I postulated some minutes ago."

"What are you talking about?" Shaw demanded brusquely. "And why are you both so pale? It's your diet, you know. With all that mutton, drink, and tobacco, you're digging yourselves early graves, the pair of you. Look at me! I haven't even a coat in this weather, and you don't see me shaking like the dickens."

"Spare us your sovereign remedies, I beg you."

"Then tell me what has happened. Did you find Wilde?"

"At the top of his form." The detective thereupon detailed for our salubrious client the encounter at the Avondale lounge and its singular aftermath in the writing room. When he mentioned the Marquess of Queensberry and spoke of Wilde's warrant, the most extraordinary change came over Shaw. He paled, leapt to his feet, and stood trembling.

"The man's taken leave of his senses!" he cried and, squeezing past, ran from the restaurant. Holmes and I stared at one another in disbelief and perplexity.

"What is going on?" I demanded, but he shrugged noncommittally.

"Our difficulties lie at Twenty-four South Crescent and the dressing room of the Savoy Theatre—not the lounge of the Avondale. At least, they don't as yet." He looked at his watch and sighed. "We are not going to run Sir Arthur to ground this evening; that much seems evident."

"He probably wouldn't enjoy it if we interrupted a game of chemin de fer played with his titled friends," * I agreed.

"And I can't say I feel very much like dining. Shall

---

* According to biographical accounts, these games, played for high stakes, frequently included the Prince of Wales.

we go? It is quite a three-pipe problem, and my cherry-wood has a larger bowl than the oily briar I am carrying. Not that I feel like smoking, either." He shook his head and started to rise. "Perhaps it's Shaw's influence."

"I think I shall remain here for a few minutes more," I said quietly.

"My dear fellow, you're not truly ill?" He pressed a hand to my brow. "You feel quite warm, but then so do I." He repeated the experiment with his own forehead. "It appears we've both caught colds."

"I'll be myself in a little," I protested, thinking the while that this was the oddest cold I'd ever contracted. "You go on and I'll catch you up."

"You're quite sure?"

He hesitated a moment or so longer, scanning my features and generally subjecting me to a close inspection before straightening up with a sigh. "Very well. Come to think of it, early to bed at Baker Street may do as well for me. Come as soon as you feel able."

I nodded heavily and he moved off. When he had gone, I sat for some time, feeling the fever take possession of my body. I drank some more water from the carafe. The waiter returned and asked if I wished to order. I told him that we had all changed our minds and started to rise. He perceived I was ill and asked if he might fetch me a cab.

"Thank you, I'll walk. The fresh air might do me good."

I got feebly to my feet and staggered out of doors, observing that it had begun to snow quite heavily again. I struck off down the street, perspiring profusely amidst the silent, frosty deluge, aware that more sensible folk had forsaken the night air in favour of a warm fire and a toasty bed.

And then something so unexpected happened that I

could scarcely credit it. I was seized from behind by a powerful pair of arms and pulled bodily out of the glare of the gas lamps into an alley that adjoined the restaurant. In my weakened condition struggle was useless. One of the gloved hands now reached 'round and held my nose, so that I could not breathe save through my mouth, whilst the other brought a vial of liquid to my lips and forced them open. It was either drink or suffocate, and I drank, perforce, my head reeling, my ears pounding, my feet slipping madly about beneath me on the icy pavement. I was unable to see either my assailant or the colour of what I was swallowing. It tasted bitter and was faintly charged with alcohol. I was obliged to drink off the entire mess and was then released. The shock of the attack and my fever combined to render me helpless. I collapsed in a darkness like oblivion, dimly conscious of the snow piling up about me.

How long I remained in that alley, I did not learn until much later. Eventually, two constables on their rounds espied me and forced some brandy down my throat. At first they supposed that I had consumed too much liquor at some earlier point in the evening, but awakening, I identified myself and related what had happened. Ascertaining that I was unable to describe my attacker, they put me in a cab and I returned to Baker Street.

There another surprise awaited me. Sherlock Holmes, in bed with pillows propping him up, informed me that upon leaving the restaurant, he too had been assaulted in the same manner.

# EIGHT

# Mama, the Crab, and Others

Breakfast the next morning at Baker Street was a subdued repast. Aside from hearing my story and telling me his—so very similar—Holmes ate in silence. In spite of my vigil in the snow, I slept well and my fever had quite vanished. With its departure my appetite reasserted itself and I made a good breakfast as we puzzled over the affair in disjointed syllables.

"It doesn't seem to have done us any harm," Holmes allowed finally.

"Rather the reverse, I should say."

He nodded and poured some more coffee. "I have known parents who cozened reluctant children into swallowing medicine in that fashion." He set aside his napkin and reached for his clay. We could neither of us begin to describe our mysterious assailant. What motive inspired him was—like so much else regarding this bizarre business—tabled for the time being, pending the accumulation of further data.

"Is it still your intention to seek out Arthur Sullivan?"

"More than ever. I'm hoping he can add to our negligible store of information regarding Jack Point. If he cannot, we shall be obliged to perform the real drudgery of detective work of the kind they do so well at Craig's Court.* By which I mean going to Miss Rutland's lodgings, talking with the neighbours, and so forth. It is the kind of refined spying that usually requires an effective disguise, for people become close-mouthed if they think you desire such information, whereas they positively press it on you if it appears you do not. Are you coming?"

"Yes, indeed."

I had started to suit action to the word and put on my jacket when a knock on the door was followed by the entrance of our landlady.

"A boy left this for you at the front door, Mr. Holmes."

"Thank you, Mrs. Hudson." He came forward and took the small brown envelope.

"May I tell the girl to clear?"

"What? Yes, yes."

Utterly absorbed, like a child with a new toy, Holmes walked over to the bow window and held the packet up to the grey sunlight.

"Hmm. No postmark, of course. Address typewritten—on a Remington in need of a new ribbon. Paper. Hmm. Paper is Indian—yes, definite watermark—no visible fingerprints—"

"Holmes, in heaven's name open it."

"In good time, my dear fellow, in good time."

He had, however, completed his examination of the envelope and now proceeded to slit open one end, using the jackknife he kept on the mantel for such purposes. He withdrew a folded sheet of the same dark stock and spread it out upon his knee.

"*Liverpool Daily Mail, Morning Courant, London*

* Craig's Court, in Whitehall, was the center of the private detective business, with no fewer than six agencies housed there.

*Times,* and the *Saturday Review,* if I am not mistaken," he murmured, running his eye over it with a practised air.

"What are you talking about?"

"The different sources for these cuttings. Here." He passed the paper to me. Its message ran:

aS you VALUE your liveS
STAY out of the Strand

There was no signature. As I looked at the message, with its arbitrary configurations of letters, scissored to reorder their sense, I thought of our adventure outside Simpson's the night before and experienced a very real tingle of fear. I have not known the sensation often, but I venture to say I am no stranger to it. I shuddered and could feel my blood running cold, as though my fever had returned. I looked up from the paper and beheld Holmes's grey eyes searching mine.

"Still game, Watson?" cried he. It was plain to see that he regarded the paper as a challenge.

"Still. Tell me, are you certain of the papers from which these words were taken?"

"You know that I am perfectly capable of identifying no fewer than twelve periodicals by their typeface," he responded with an injured look.

"Then does the printing itself suggest nothing to you?"

"Beyond the fact that the writer wishes to remain anonymous, very little." His eyes twinkled. "What does it suggest to you?"

"Why look at the sources he has used!" I cried with some excitement. "The *Morning Courant* and the *Saturday Review.* Does that not bring us back to my theory of a deadly rivalry between those two papers?"

"Say, does it not rather steer us away from your theory? Only a fool, in the position in which you place our man, would compose his message with either of the typefaces at issue. And then, how does your theory explain the murder of poor Miss Rutland?"

"It fails to," I admitted ruefully. "At the moment. But what do you make of Shaw's bolting out of the restaurant like that? Where does that fit in your precious triangle?"

"Do you imply that it was Shaw who waited outside and initiated the curious attacks?"

"He hasn't the strength for it, obviously. Besides, we have no way of determining if the attacks were even related to this business."

Holmes threw on his coat. "I should be surprised to learn that they were not, and so should you; come, confess it. No, my dear doctor, I fancy our correspondent merely chose the words he required where he chanced upon them. The *Courant* and the *Review,* after all, are both prominent sheets. Come along."

On our way to the Lyceum, we read the morning papers in the cab. There was a brief piece on the warrant sworn out by Wilde against the Marquess of Queensberry, as well as quite a detailed account (on another page) of the murder at 24 South Crescent. Heavy emphasis was placed on the pronouncements of Inspector G. Lestrade, who promised to "lay the culprit by the heels" in "very short order" and who described the critic's murderer for the benefit of the press in a neat paraphrase of Sherlock Holmes's own summation.

Holmes chuckled as he ran over the account. "There are some comforting consistencies in this reeling world of ours, Watson," said he, "and Lestrade must be accounted one of them. The man hasn't changed a hair in the last dozen years."

"The paper nowhere makes mention of Miss Rutland," I noted.

"Quite possibly not. I believe the *Times* goes to bed too early in the evening, but we shall find it, no doubt, in this afternoon's edition. The murderer will have the dubious satisfaction of seeing himself in print twice in one day."

"You're convinced it is the same man, then?"

"I think it would be stretching coincidence if it were not. Besides, he has the same style—and shoes."

"I was not aware of any great similarity between the crimes. Quite the contrary, the first appears to have been committed on impulse, whereas the second obviously involved a deal of premeditation."

"That is true. It is also true, however, that in both cases a knife-like weapon was employed—how fittingly McCarthy referred to him in his diary as Jack Point!—and in both cases the man displayed a more than rudimentary knowledge of anatomy. Indeed, his throat-slitting was accomplished with surgical precision and must have dispatched his second victim with humane immediacy."

"Humane!"

"Well, relatively."

"How do you reconcile the crime of impulse with the crime of premeditation?"

"I do not reconcile them as yet, but I will advance a provisional theory: Jack Point, our discarded lover, in talking with Jonathan McCarthy for whatever reason, learns of the latter's infatuation. In a rage of impulse he slays the man, and in one of forethought, he revenges himself upon his faithless mistress. Ah, here is the Lyceum!"

We stepped out of the cab before the imposing columns of that reverend structure. Like a man in a trance, I advanced to the third pillar from the left.

"Are you all right, Watson? I had forgotten."

"I think so." I hesitated for some moments, leaning against the pillar, my eyes filling with tears. It was to this column, some seven years before, that Holmes and I accompanied young Mary Morstan, my future wife, on the errand of intrigue which first brought her to our door.* It was now almost three years since her untimely death, and I had never, in all that time, found myself so near the starting point of our great adventure together. With an effort I regained my composure and indicated that I was ready to proceed.

The front doors of the Lyceum were open, and we stepped into the elegant foyer.

"Can I help you?" The deep voice which spoke these words startled us, the more so as we could not determine whence it came. The mystery was quickly solved when the shuttered windows of the box office were banged open and we were confronted by a dark, bearded man with a pinched aquiline nose and expressionless black eyes. He sat behind a set of bars like a teller's window, and my first thought was that he should stay behind them.

"Can I help you?" he repeated with the same wooden inflection.

"We are looking for Sir Arthur Sullivan," Holmes explained. "Is he here this morning? We were told he would be."

"Who wants to know?"

"Mr. Sherlock Holmes."

The bearded apparition remained stock-still at these words, then rose with startling decision and slammed the shutters. In another moment the door to the box office opened and he strode out, a man just under six feet, wearing a dark, impeccably tailored suit,

---

* Details of the case may be found in Watson's second opus, *The Sign of the Four*.

which failed to conceal a powerful, not to say athletic physique.

"Sherlock Holmes?" His bottomless black eyes travelled from one to the other of us. Holmes inclined his head slightly.

"You wish to see Sir Arthur? He is occupied with Sir Henry. Can I help you with something?" There was no warmth behind the offer.

"You can help me to Sir Arthur," Holmes answered, undismayed by the man's threatening visage. "And you may pay my compliments to John Henry Brodribb."

He blinked as though a riding crop had been swung before his face. It was his only human response thus far. Without further comment he spun on his heel and entered the theatre.

"What a singular personage. I declare, Holmes, there doesn't seem to be a sane individual connected with this profession."

"There was a time when decent hotels wouldn't put them up," he agreed, "and it used to be a commonplace to observe that an actor shot President Lincoln." He pursed his lips, trying to recall something. "Did that man say 'Sir Henry'? Surely not."

I was about to reply to this with some speculation of my own when the clatter of horses' hooves upon the cobblestones outside the theatre attracted our attention.

A brougham had driven up, and out of it there stepped the prettiest woman I can remember ever having seen. Her figure was trim and girlish, though I saw when she drew close, that she must be nearing fifty. Nevertheless, her hair was blonde beneath a rakishly tilted hat and her eyes a radiant blue. Her nose was diminutive but not without nobility and was set above an expressive, humourous mouth. When she smiled—which was often—I caught a glimpse of perfect white teeth that shone like ropes of pearls. It was not her features individually, however, that provoked admiration, but rather the *tout ensemble* created by the engaging intellect that yoked them together. An air of healthy common sense and warmth pervaded, in distinct contrast to the last person we had seen in this lobby. What a place of extremes!

The woman descending from the brougham blew a kiss to the coachman (of all things!) and danced into the foyer.

"Good morning!" she called cheerily, noticing us. "Tickets do not go on sale before noon, you know— though you are quite right to be here early; they've been going like hot cakes all week!"

"Have I the honour of addressing Miss Ellen Terry?" Holmes smiled.

The ravishing creature returned his smile and responded to his bow with a lithesome curtsey.

"You look familiar, too, if you don't mind my saying so," she replied. "Have you been an actor?"

"Not for many years—on the stage, that is. But once, long ago, I trod the boards with John Henry Brodribb." Her eyes went wide with astonishment, and she burst into a peal of girlish laughter.

"No! You acted with the Crab before he *was* the Crab? You don't look old enough to have done any such thing," she challenged playfully.

"I assure you, I wasn't. I was eight at the time and played a page during a performance of *Hamlet* at York. My parents discovered me from the audience and were thoroughly appalled." *

"But this is wonderful! Does he know you are here to see him? He will be so amused! Oh, but I'm afraid

---

* This placing of Holmes in the vicinity of York when he was eight years old seems to corroborate Baring-Gould's biography, in which the detective's childhood in Donninthorpe is described.

he may be dreadfully busy just now. Revivals are so trying. We're attempting to recall what we did with *Macbeth* when we got it right the first time." *

"There was a dark-haired, bearded gentleman here a moment ago. I believe he has gone upon my errand."

"Oh, you've met Mama."

"I beg your pardon?"

"You must forgive my penchant"—she pronounced it as though it were a French word—"for nicknames. Irving says I'm quite incorrigible."

"Irving, I take it, is the Crab?"

"But of course!" she giggled mischievously. "Oh, but you mustn't say I said so. He's terribly sensitive about the way he walks."

"And Mama?"

"That is Mr. Stoker, our business manager and general secretary. He is so very protective of us all that I call him Mama."

"Bram Stoker?"

"Why, yes. Do you know him, as well? I don't know either of your names," she realised suddenly, with another laugh, "and here I've been gossiping as though we were all old friends."

"Forgive me. My name is Sherlock Holmes, and this is my friend, Dr. Watson."

"*Now* I know why you looked familiar!" She clapped her gloved hands together delightedly. "I've seen your likenesses in the *Strand* magazine, haven't I?" She laughed at having placed us, then stopped short. "Are you here on business?"

"In a way, though my business is with Sir Arthur Sullivan, not with Sir Henry."

"Oh, you mustn't call him that yet, you know; it's

* Irving first produced *Macbeth* in 1888.

two months off.* Mama does it, of course—he's so
fond of titles—but it drives Irving quite wild. With
Sullivan, is it?" She frowned, tapping her foot, then
smiled with resolution. "Well, come with me, and
I'll see if we can't beard the pair of 'em." She turned
to enter the theatre when the door opened suddenly
and Stoker reappeared. Miss Terry gave a little shriek
of fright, then laughed again, placing a hand on her
bosom.

"How you startled me, Bram!"

"I beg your pardon," said he stiffly. From the suddenness with which he opened the door, I suspected
him of having eavesdropped on a considerable portion of the conversation. "Sir Arthur will see you
now," he informed us coldly.

"I'll take them, thank you, Bram."

"They're in the Club Room, Ellen." He stood to
one side, holding the door to let us pass, bowing low
to the lady with what I thought exaggerated formality.
We entered the theatre and started down the aisle in
her wake.

"Dear Mama," she commented.

The Lyceum, which I had not seen for some time,
was a theatre lavish beyond belief and famed for the
unstinting artistic effort and money that went into its
productions. Confronting us on the stage as we walked
towards it was a stunning rendition of what I took to
be the blasted heath which opens *Macbeth*. Real trees
were in evidence, as well as shrubbery and a three-
dimensional rocky terrain. The effect was so startling
that we stopped for a moment in wonder.

"Isn't it remarkable?" Miss Terry remarked. "Sir
Edward Burne-Jones does a great many of our productions. Sometimes I think the public comes here just to
look at the sets."

* Henry Irving was knighted two months later by Queen
Victoria, the first of his profession to be so honored.

"What is the Club Room?" I asked as we went through a side door and entered the complicated backstage portion of the theatre. All around us carpenters were hammering, sawing, and yelling instructions to one another, obliging us to shout over the din.

"Ah, that is Irving's pride and joy. Samuel Arnold,* the composer, who built the first Lyceum— predecessor of this theatre—added it years ago for his Sublime Society of Beefsteaks. Sheridan was a member, you know! And Irving has restored it. There's a kitchen, and he so loves to entertain and relax after a performance. Here we are." She stopped before a door that gave out from the back of the building.

"It seems to me I have met Mr. Stoker before," Holmes remarked offhandedly. "Doesn't he live in Soho?" Ellen Terry spun around, her finger to her lips.

"Hush! Oh, please, *please,* you mustn't mention anything of the kind in there. It was such a sore point when it happened the first time! I don't know that Irving's ever forgiven him for it, and that was years ago."

"What do you mean? Is he—?"

"Hush, I *beg* you, Mr. Holmes!" She put her head to the door and listened intently, then with a little smirk, signed for us to do the same. Despite her advancing years, she had the disposition and energy of a very young girl. Following her instructions, we put our heads to the door.

"No, no, no, my dear chap!" came an odd-sounding deep voice, very nasal. "As music, it may be all very well, but it's not right for our purpose at all. Listen! I *see* the daggers, and I want them *heard* by the audience."

---

* The great-grandfather of Edgar Allan Poe.

"But, Henry, what do daggers sound like?" a high-pitched voice protested in a slight whine.

"What do they sound like? They sound like—" And then we heard the queerest succession of grunts and growls, alternately sounding like squeaks and a beehive.

"Oh, yes, yes! I see what you mean! That's much better!" the high, piping voice exclaimed. "Yes, I think I can do that."

"Good."

Miss Terry, having amused herself sufficiently, knocked peremptorily on the door and opened it without waiting for a response.

"I'm sorry to disturb you, my dears," she adopted a business-like, matter-of-fact tone, "but here are the two gentlemen who wished to see Sir Arthur." What a little actress she was!

The spacious quarters into which we were shown indeed suggested an ideal retreat after a strenuous night's work in the theatre. Dominating the place was a long oak table at which thirty guests might easily put in a pleasant hour or two over several cold birds and bottles.

At the far end of the table, beneath portraits of David Garrick and Edmund Kean, two figures sat cloistered together, looking like conspirators interrupted in the midst of an anarchist plot.

The taller of the two was a melancholy man in his late fifties, with cavernously hollow cheeks, long grey hair, piercing eyes of an indeterminate colour, and a studiously grave demeanour. He rose courteously and bowed as we entered. Over his shoulders was carelessly draped a massive maroon cloak, which lent to his distinguished appearance an appropriately theatrical touch.

Sir Arthur Sullivan rose, as well. He was not nearly so tall as Henry Irving, nor as dramatic in his costume. He wore his expensive clothes unaffectedly, as one who is used to fine things, and though a trifle stout, was possessed of dark, slightly Semitic good looks. His sad eyes were a lustrous brown and reminded me forcibly of a cow's as they peered myopically through the pince-nez that rested familiarly on the bridge of his nose. Like Gilbert, he affected large sidewhiskers, and their effect, I judged, was to make him seem older than he really was. He held his right hand at an unnatural angle throughout our conversation, pressing it against his stomach. Altogether there was in his face and in his bearing that which did not suggest a healthy man.

"Gentlemen," said Irving in his odd nasal voice, "we are sorry to have kept you waiting."

"And we are equally sorry to interrupt your business."

"I've been with the police most of the morning," Sullivan informed us sadly as we shook hands. "I don't know what I can say to you that I haven't told them. May I ask at whose behest you come to see me?"

Suddenly he gasped and clutched spasmodically at his side, turning quite pale. Irving caught him tenderly as he stumbled, breaking the fall, and gently lowered him into a chair. He whispered his thanks to the actor, then turned, catching his breath, and repeated his question.

"We are here at the behest of justice," Holmes informed him, ignoring, for the moment, his seizure. "More prosaically, we were asked to look into the matter by Mr. Bernard Shaw."

The reaction of the two men to this piece of intelligence was startling. Sullivan knit his brows, perplexed, while Irving straightened up abruptly, his face clouding over, rendering his appearance more sombre than it was already.

"Shaw?" he cried, his courtly attitude slipping a

little as he darted a glance at Ellen Terry. "Nellie, is this any of your doing?"

"Henry, dearest, I give you my word I know nothing about it," Miss Terry replied, obviously taken aback. "I met these gentlemen only moments ago in the lobby."

Irving started ominously down the length of the table. As he walked—or rather, shuffled—I was struck by his manner of thrusting his right shoulder forward, and I had to smile at Miss Terry's pet name for him.

"I give you warning, Nellie—" he spoke at the door—"I give you fair warning. I will not have that degenerate in this theatre—"

"He's not a degenerate, Henry. What are you talking about?" she spoke up with spirit. Irving went on as though he hadn't heard.

"I will not have him in this theatre, and I will not produce his revolting plays. And if he publishes any more drivel about the way we do things here, I will thrash him personally."

"Henry," she protested, looking anxiously around him at us and smiling nervously, "this is not the time or the place—"

"Let him stay at the Court with Granville Barker, where he belongs," Irving grumbled, calming somewhat. "Where they *all* belong. I don't want him or his plays here. Is that understood?" *

"Yes, Henry," said she meekly. "Come along and let's leave these gentlemen to their business."

This recalled the actor to himself and he turned to us with another bow.

* This reference to the Court Theatre is mystifying as it anticipates events by many years. Perhaps Watson's memory plays him false here. Then again, it may be this editor's mistake as the water damage suffered by the manuscript is particularly severe at this point. Nonetheless, it *does* look like "the Court with Granville Barker," etcetera.

"I apologise for my outburst, gentlemen. I know I am sometimes carried away. The theatre in this country will go in one of two directions shortly, and I feel quite strongly about which it's to be."

He spoke simply and with such evident feeling that, strangers to his ideas, we lowered our heads, embarrassed and, I think, moved by the display of raw emotion.

"Come, Henry." He allowed her to lead him from the room, a wearying Titan, I thought, following a Dresden shepherdess, herself no longer young.

Alone now with the composer, we turned and faced him.

# NINE

# Sullivan

"Were you really sent 'round by Bernard Shaw?" Sullivan began testily when the door was closed. "Why is he meddling in this? The man's an infernal busybody, and aside from his knowledge of music, I find him utterly depraved."

"He did not engage us specifically in the matter of Miss Rutland," Holmes acknowledged, moving forward and pulling up one of the large chairs, "but rather in connection with the murder of Jonathan McCarthy."

Wincing at another spasm, the composer screwed himself 'round in his seat and faced the detective.

"That makes still less sense, if I may say so, since they detested each other."

"A great many people appear to have disliked Jonathan McCarthy, that is certain."

"Granted, granted. Shaw's tongue may be wicked, but he always addresses himself to the issues. McCarthy was a parasite, preying on art and artists, which is not the same thing." He started to rise, gave another gasp, and fell back in his chair, doubled over and clutching at his side as though he wished to remove it in one savage haul. His pince-nez slid from his nose and dangled wildly by its black ribbon, inches from the floor.

"You are seriously ill!" I cried, rushing forward. For several moments he was unable to answer but lay gasping in his chair, like a fish out of water. I opened his tie for him and removed his collar. I perceived the kitchen Ellen Terry had spoken of and hastened to it for some water, which I brought back to him. He swallowed it in awkward gulps.

"Thank you."

"You are too ill to continue this interview," I stated, drawing a black look across the table from Holmes.

Sir Arthur sat up slowly. Something that resembled a smile stretched itself taut across his face. "Ill? I am dying. These kidney stones are working their way with me and will shortly make an end." He shrugged feebly and replaced his pince-nez. "When the pain disappears, I go to Monte Carlo and relax; when it returns, I work to forget it. I am in London, working; ergo, it is back." *

"Can you continue talking?" Holmes enquired reluctantly.

"I can and I will, provided you establish the importance of your questions." Sullivan rallied and sat straighter in his chair, re-fastening his collar with nervous little fingers.

"Do you not find the fact that both murders occurred within the space of twenty-four hours a telling coincidence?"

"Inspector Lestrade didn't appear to find it so. He didn't even mention the McCarthy affair when we talked this morning."

"The police have their own ways of functioning,"

---

* Sullivan succumbed to his ailment five years later.

Holmes stated tactfully. "And I have mine. I may tell you flatly that the deaths are related."

"How so?"

"They were achieved by the same hand."

Sullivan smiled faintly. "I have read Dr. Watson's accounts of your cases with the liveliest interest," he confessed, "and have always found them agreeably stimulating. Nevertheless, you will forgive me if, in this instance, I do not deem your word sufficient proof."

Holmes sighed, realising that Sullivan was no fool. He would have to play more of the cards in his hand.

"Were you aware, Sir Arthur, that Jessie Rutland was Jonathan McCarthy's mistress?" The composer blanched as though his fatal ailment had flared up again.

"That's impossible!" he retorted with heat. "She was no such thing."

"I assure you that she was." Holmes leaned forward earnestly, his eyes bright. "Our informant, whom I am not yet at liberty to disclose, assures me that she was. His accuracy in several other small matters forces me to trust him in this, the more so as it provides an otherwise missing link between these two crimes."

"What small matters?"

"For one thing, he states flatly that a leading member of the Savoy company uses drugs because Mr. Gilbert makes him so nervous."

"That is a damned lie." But he spoke without conviction and subsided into thoughtful silence. Holmes surveyed him coolly for a few moments, then leaned forward again.

"A moment ago you violently resisted the idea of Jonathan McCarthy as Jessie Rutland's lover. It wasn't merely because you despised the man. You *knew* better, didn't you?"

"It seems pointless now."

The grey eyes of Sherlock Holmes grew brighter than ever; they burned like twin beacons.

"I give you my word it is of the utmost moment. Jessie Rutland is dead; we cannot restore her to life or confer upon her any advantages, save, possibly, a decent funeral. But there is one thing we can do, and that is to bring her murderer to book."

It was now Sullivan's turn to study Holmes, and this he did for what seemed like a solid minute, glaring at him through his pince-nez, without moving, his hand pressed to his side. "Very well. What do you want to know?"

The detective breathed an imperceptible sigh of relief. "Tell us about Jack Point."

"Who?"

"Forgive me, that is the name by which McCarthy referred to him in his engagement calendar. He appears to have made a practise of substituting characters from your operas for the real names of people. The appointment in his diary for the night of his death was with Jack Point. Point is the hapless jester who loses his love in *Yeomen of the Guard,* is he not?"

"He is! He is!" Sullivan was impressed by the detective's familiarity with his work. "So you think Jessie had a second lover?"

"You've as good as told me she had, Sir Arthur."

Sullivan frowned, reached into his breast pocket, and withdrew a cigarette case. He extracted a cigarette, tapped it several times in a nervous tattoo against the box, then allowed Holmes to light it for him, throwing his head back gratefully as he blew out a cloud of smoke.

"You must understand first that Gilbert runs the Savoy," he began. "He runs it like a military outpost, with the strictest discipline, on stage and off. You may have observed that the men's and women's dressing rooms are on opposite sides of the stage. Congregation betwixt them is strictly forbidden. Conduct of the company while in the theatre—and to a very great degree outside of it—must satisfy Gilbert's mania for propriety.

"If his attitude seems to you gentlemen somewhat extreme, let me say that I understand and sympathise with what he has been trying to accomplish. The reputation of actresses has never been a very good one. The word itself has for many years been accepted as a synonym for something rather worse. Mr. Gilbert is attempting at the Savoy to expunge that particular synonym. His methods may seem severe and ludicrous at times, and—" he hesitated, tapping an ash— "individuals may suffer, but in the long run, I believe, he will have performed a useful service.

"Now, as to Jessie Rutland. I engaged her three years ago and never had any cause to regret my decision. She was, I knew, an orphan, raised in Woking, who had sung in various church choirs. She had no family nor income of her own. Gaining a position at the Savoy meant everything to her. For the first time in her life, she not only earned a decent wage, she had a home, a family, a place to which she belonged, and she was grateful for it."

He stopped, momentarily overcome, whether by mental or physical anguish it was impossible to say.

"Go on," Holmes ordered. His eyes were closed and the tips of his fingers pressed together beneath his chin—his customary attitude when listening.

"She was a dear child, very pretty, with a lovely soprano—a little coarse in the middle range, but that would have improved with time and practise. She was a hard worker and a willing one, always ready to do as she was told.

"My contact with the theatre is generally of the slightest. I engage the singers after auditioning them, and as the songs are written, I play them over for the company and soloists until they are learned. And I conduct on opening nights if I am able." He smiled grimly. "Mr. Grossmith is not the only member of the company who has used drugs to get through a performance."

"I am no stranger to them myself, Sir Arthur. Please continue."

"Normally, Mr. Cellier rehearses the chorus and soloists. It was a surprise to me, therefore, when several weeks ago, Jessie approached me after a rehearsal in which I had gone over some new material with the chorus, and asked if she might speak with me privately, as she was in need of advice. She was clearly distressed, and looking at her closely, I perceived that she had been weeping.

"My first impulse was to refer her to Gilbert. He is much more popular with the company than I—" this stated with a wistful air—"for though he sometimes tyrannises them and plays the martinet, they know he loves them and has their interests very much at heart, whereas I am a relative stranger. When I suggested this course of action to her, however, she started to cry again, saying that it was impossible.

" 'If I confide in Mr. Gilbert, I am lost!' she cried. 'I will lose my place, and *he* will be harmed, as well!' " The composer sighed and dusted an imaginary speck of ash off his sleeve. "I am a busy man, Mr. Holmes, with many demands upon my time, both musical and otherwise." He coughed and put out his cigarette, his eyes avoiding our own. "Nevertheless, I was touched by the girl's appeal and I agreed to listen to her story. We met the next afternoon at a little teashop in the Marylebone Road. We were not likely to be recognized there, or if we were, it would be difficult to place any sordid construction on our presence.

" 'Tell me,' I said, when we had given our order.

'Tell me what has upset you.' 'I will not take up your time with preliminaries,' said she. 'Recently I made the acquaintance of a gentleman to whom I have become most attached. He is quite perfect in every way, and his behaviour towards myself has never been less than proper. Knowing the stringent rules governing conduct at the Savoy, we have behaved with the utmost circumspection. But, oh, Sir Arthur, he is so very perfect that even Mr. Gilbert must have approved! I have fallen in love!' she cried, 'and so has he!' 'But my dear,' I responded warmly, 'this is no cause for tears. You are to be congratulated! As for Mr. Gilbert, I give you my word of honour he will dance at your wedding!'

"At this point, Mr. Holmes, she began to cry in the midst of the restaurant, though she did her best to conceal the fact by holding a small cambric handkerchief before her face. 'There can be no wedding,' she sobbed, 'because he is already married. That is what he has just told me.' 'If he has deceived you in this fashion,' I retorted, much surprised, 'then he is utterly unworthy of your affections and you are well rid of him.' 'You don't understand,' said she, regaining her composure, 'he has not deceived me—as you mean. His wife is an invalid, confined to a nursing home in Bombay. She—' "

"One moment," Sherlock Holmes broke in, opening his eyes. "Did she say 'Bombay'?"

"Yes."

"Pray continue." His eyes closed again.

" 'His wife can neither hear nor speak nor walk,' she told me, 'as she was the victim of a stroke five years ago. Nevertheless, he is chained to her.' She was unable to suppress a trace of bitterness as she spoke, though I could not at the time—nor can I now—find it in my heart to reproach her for it. 'He feared to tell me of his plight,' she went on, 'for fear of losing me. Yet when he saw the direction our affections were

SULLIVAN

taking, he knew he must disclose the truth. And now I don't know what to do!' she concluded and pulled forth her handkerchief yet again while I sat across the small table from her and pondered.

"Mr. Holmes, you can imagine how I felt. The woman had placed me in a most delicate position. I am part owner of the Savoy and in theory, at least, sympathise with Mr. Gilbert's aspirations for its company; thus, my duties clearly lay in one direction. But I am a human being and, moreover, a man who has experienced a very similar problem,* and so my emotions and personal inclinations lay in quite another."

"What did you advise?"

He looked at the detective without flinching. "I advised her to follow her heart. Oh, I know what you will say, but we are only here once, Mr. Holmes—at least, that is my conviction—and I believe we should seize what chance of happiness we can. I told her I would not reveal her secret to Mr. Gilbert, and I was as good as my word, but I warned her that I could not shield her from the consequences should he learn of her intrigue from another source."

"I begin to understand a little," said Holmes, "though there is much that remains obscure. Did she say anything at all concerning her young man that would enable us to identify him?"

"She was most careful to avoid doing so. The closest she came to an indiscretion was to let slip that the wife's nursing home was in Bombay. I am quite certain she made no other reference."

"I see." Holmes closed his eyes briefly and tapped his fingertips together. "And how much of all this did you tell the police this morning?"

The composer blushed and dropped his eyes.

* Sullivan's mistress was an American, Mrs. Ronalds, who was separated but not divorced. They remained devoted to one another throughout much of his life.

"Not a word?" Holmes was unable to conceal a trace of scorn. "The woman cannot now be compromised, surely. She has no place to lose."

"But I, *I* can be compromised," the other responded softly. "If it emerges that I knew of a liaison at the Savoy and failed to mention it to Gilbert—" He sighed. "Relations between us have never been very cordial, and of late they have become more strained than usual. He has never got over the fact of my knighthood, you know. But we need each other, Mr. Holmes!" He laughed shortly and without mirth. "The ironic truth is that we cannot function apart. Oh, I grant you 'The Lost Chord' and 'The Golden Legend,' but when all is said and done, I have the hideous knowledge that my forte is *The Mikado* and others of that ilk. He knows it, too, and knows that it is for our Savoy operas, if anything, that we shall be remembered. I have not long to live," he concluded, "but while I breathe, I cannot afford to antagonise him further."

"I understand you, Sir Arthur, and I apologise for having seemed to pass judgement. One final question." Sullivan looked up.

"Do you know Bram Stoker's wife?"

The question took him by surprise, but he recovered and shrugged. "His wife is a good friend of Gilbert's, I believe. That is all I can tell you."

Holmes rose. "Thank you for your time. Come, Watson."

"I trust you will be discreet—if possible," Sullivan murmured as we moved towards the door.

"Discretion is a part of my profession. By the way—" Holmes hesitated, his hand on the knob. "I saw *Ivanhoe*." *

---

* *Ivanhoe* was Sullivan's sole excursion into the realm of grand opera. It was not generally accounted successful.

Sullivan looked at him over the rim of his pince-nez. "Oh?"

"I quite liked it."

"Really? That's more than I did." He stared moodily at the table top before him as Holmes opened the door.

Bram Stoker was standing there.

"Did you observe his boots?" the detective murmured softly after we had passed.

# TEN

# The Man with Brown Eyes

Sherlock Holmes refused to elaborate on his observation regarding Bram Stoker's boots, the man's eavesdropping, or Ellen Terry's reaction to his enquiry after Stoker's Soho flat. Indeed, he declined to volunteer any thoughts upon leaving the Lyceum.

"Later, Watson," said he as we stood on the kerb before the theatre. "Things are not so simple as I had first supposed."

I was about to ask him what he meant by this when he took me by the sleeve.

"I must spend the afternoon in some research, Doctor. Might I prevail upon you to assist me in a small matter?"

"Anything you like."

"I want you to find Bernard Shaw and learn the meaning of his eccentric behaviour last night."

"You begin to attach some importance to my theory, then?"

"It may be," he answered, smiling. "At all events, I think it would be as well to have all the threads of this tangled skein in our hands. It is almost lunchtime, and I fancy you will come upon him at the Café Royal. I know he likes to take his meals there. Good luck."

He squeezed my arm and started rapidly down the street.

"Where shall we meet?" I called after him.

"Baker Street."

When he had rounded the corner, I wasted no time but hailed a cab and hastened directly to the Café Royal, a snow-bound mile from the Lyceum. Indeed, all the events in which we found ourselves immersed at present had taken place within the space of a single square mile, a thought which made me pause as I considered it. The world of the theatre proved to be more insular than any I had heretofore encountered. All denizens of that world appeared to know one another at least slightly, creating an atmosphere so domestically intimate that in it a single sneeze would likely be overheard by a thousand people.

The Café Royal was crowded when I entered, and, it seemed to me, in a collective state of some confusion. Nervous clusters of people whispered intently together, huddling 'round tables and glancing apprehensively over their shoulders.

"Doctor!"

I peered about at the agitated throng and beheld Bernard Shaw, seated at a table with another man, whose coarse appearance disturbed me at once. He was short and squat, with eyes too closely set on either side of a prizefighter's pug nose, and his head sat awkwardly atop a thick, muscular neck, which threatened to burst the confines of his collar and tie.

"This is Mr. Harris," the critic informed me as I joined them, dropping into a chair opposite. "He's one of our leading publishers. We are here commiserating. The whole place is," he added sardonically, looking about. "And speculating."

"About what?"

They looked at one another briefly.

"About Oscar Wilde's folly," boomed Mr. Harris

111

in a voice designed to be heard across the room. My face must have betrayed my confusion.

"You recall my running out of Simpson's last night, Doctor, I've no doubt?" enquired Shaw.

"I could hardly help remarking upon it at the time."

He grunted and stirred his coffee with a disinterested motion, leaning his cheek upon an open palm. "It was the beginning of a horrible night. In the first place, some maniac assaulted me outside the restaurant."

"Assaulted you?" I could feel the blood quickening in my veins and the hairs rising on the back of my neck.

"Some kind of practical joke, but it served to delay me when I thought speed counted most. I was trying to prevent the arrest of the Marquess of Queensberry. I rushed right here—to this very booth!—and sat with Frank here, doing my best to dissuade him."

"Wilde?"

He nodded.

"We bent his ear," the publisher agreed in a stentorian bellow, "but it was no use. He sat through it like a man in a trance." *

Harris's accent was impossible to place, partially owing to the volume at which he spoke. It sounded alternately Welsh, Irish, and American. Later I learned that his background was much in dispute.

"He cannot prove he has been libelled?" I asked.

"It's worse than that," Shaw explained. "According to the law—which, as Mr. Bumble noted, is an ass—he leaves himself open for Queensberry to prove he hasn't."

* According to Harris, who is not reliable, and Shaw (who is), Lord Alfred Douglas was also present at this interview. "Bosie," in later years, confirmed this himself. For authoritative biographies of Shaw, Wilde, and Gilbert and Sullivan the reader is urged to consult the works of Hesketh Pearson.

"The Marquess was arrested this morning," Harris concluded in a dull rumble.

They returned glumly to their coffee, leaving me to ponder this. I wondered if I dared turn the conversation backwards and decided to attempt it: "What of your assault? I take it you were not injured?"

"Oh, that." Shaw wiggled his fingers airily. "Some kind of practical joke. I was seized from behind, forced to swallow some disagreeable concoction and then released. Can you imagine such nonsense? Right in the heart of London!" He shook his head at the thought of it, but his mind was clearly elsewhere.

"Did you get a look at the man? I assume it was one man?"

"I tell you I was paying no attention, Doctor! I simply wanted to be let go and do what I could to prevent Wilde's destroying himself. In that I failed," he added with a sigh.

"It is a foregone conclusion, then, that he will lose the case?"

"Utterly foregone," replied Harris. "Oscar Wilde, the greatest literary light of his time—" I noticed Shaw winced slightly at this—"and in three months—" Harris held up his fingers—"in three months, less, perhaps, he will be in total eclipse. People will fear to speak his name except in derision." He intoned all this as though delivering a sermon; clearly, he did not know how to speak below a roar. Yet for all his vocal posturing, I sensed a very real distress on his part.

"I should not be surprised if some of his works are proscribed," Shaw added. "Maybe all."

At the time I could not understand how grave the issue was. But in three months Frank Harris's prophecy had fulfilled itself utterly and Oscar Wilde was sent to prison for two years, his glorious career in ashes.

Ignorant of the facts surrounding the case, my mind returned to the matter at hand, and looking up at me,

Shaw perceived my train of thought. "Well, but how's the murder?" he enquired with a rueful smile, as much to say, "Here's a more cheerful topic."

"It's two murders, as I expect you'll discover in this afternoon's editions," I said and told them of the events at the Savoy Theatre, pointing out to Shaw that if he had not bolted from the restaurant the previous evening, he should have known of them earlier.

They listened to my recital, open-mouthed.

"Murder at the Savoy!" Harris gasped when I had done. "What is happening? Is the entire fabric of our community to be rent by scandal and horror within the narrow space of four days?" Somehow he managed to convey the impression of relishing the prospect. He was certainly a contradictory character.

"It begins to resemble something of Shakespeare's," Shaw agreed slowly, his sharp tongue for once at a loss. "Corpses and what-not strewn over the entire West End."

"Does either of you gentlemen know Bram Stoker?"

They looked at me, confused by the turn the talk had taken.

"Why d'ye want to know?" Harris asked.

"I don't, but Sherlock Holmes does."

"What about him?"

"That is the question I am putting to you."

Shaw hesitated, regarding me and then exchanging glances with his publisher.

"He's an odd one, all right," Harris allowed, playing with his coffee spoon. "His name isn't Bram, of course. It's Abraham."

"Indeed. What else?"

"He was born in Dublin or thereabouts, I believe, and has an older brother who is a prominent physician."

"Not Dr. William Stoker?"

114

Shaw nodded. "The same. He's due for a knighthood this spring."

"And what of Bram?"

He hunched his shoulders, then dropped them. "Athletic champion of Dublin University."

"What was his occupation before entering Irving's employ?"

The Irishman chuckled and looked something like his usual elfin self.

"All roads lead to Rome, Doctor. He was a drama critic."

"A critic?" I dimly perceived a pattern to Holmes's suspicions.

"And sometime author—of the frustrated variety."

"Did he know Jonathan McCarthy?"

"Everyone knew Jonathan McCarthy."

"And his wife is a friend of Gilbert's."

Shaw's and Harris's eyes widened.

"Where did you come to learn that?" asked Shaw.

I stood up and did my best not to appear smug. "I have my methods."

"You're not leaving, surely," Harris protested. "You've had nothing to eat."

"I'm afraid my business takes me elsewhere. Thank you, gentlemen. I hope the affair with your friend does not end as badly as you fear."

"It will end worse," Shaw muttered, shaking my hand without conviction.

Leaving them, I hastened to Baker Street, eager to impart the results of my interview to Holmes, but he had not returned. I spent a dreary afternoon pacing about the place, energetically trying to make sense out of our data and to reconcile the pieces of our puzzle into a coherent whole. At times I thought I had mastered the thing, only to recollect an item of importance which I had omitted in my latest calculations. Finally, bored with fruitless speculation,

I set about putting away the scores of books which still littered our floor, reasoning that my companion had for the moment lost interest in them.

I fell asleep at some point during my exertions, for the next thing I recall was being roused from an armchair reverie by the familiar knock of our landlady.

"There's a gentleman asking to see Mr. Holmes," she informed me.

"He isn't here, Mrs. Hudson, as you know."

"Yes, Doctor, but he says his business is most urgent, and he asked me to bring him to you."

"Urgent, is it? Very well, show him up. Stay, Mrs. Hudson, what's he like?"

The good woman frowned, then regarded me cannily. "He says he's an estate agent, sir; certainly he's well fed and wined—if you take my meaning." She tapped the side of her nose suggestively with a forefinger.

"I do indeed. Very well."

I had not long to wait before there was a second rap on the door, preceded by much huffing and puffing on the stair.

"Come in."

The door opened to admit a gentleman of advancing years and enormous girth; he must have weighed close to nineteen stone, and his every move was accompanied by gasps of effort.

"Your—very—humble—ah, servant, Doctor," he wheezed, presenting his card with a feeble flourish. It identified him as Hezekiah Jackson, of Plymouth, estate agent. The place fitted his accent, which was Devonshire in the extreme. I glanced and took in the beefy, corpulent, puffing countenance of Mr. Jackson. His bulbous nose was almost as red as a beet and the veins running over its tip as pronounced as a map of the Nile delta. They declared Mr. Jackson to be a tippler of no mean proportions. His wheezing breath

116

tended to confirm that declaration, as it was liberally laced with alcohol. His brown eyes had a glazed, staring look as they endeavoured to take in their surroundings. Perspiration glistened on his cheeks and forehead, dribbling down from his close-cropped white hair. In another age he would have been the King of Misrule.

"Mr. Jackson?" said I. "Pray have a chair."

"Thank you, sir, I don't mind if I do." He looked around, swaying on his feet, for a seat large enough to accommodate his bulk. He chose the stuffed leather by the fire, which Holmes preferred, and squeezed into it so heavily that it creaked alarmingly. I shuddered to think of the detective's response should he return and find it exploded by this obese character.

"I am Dr.—"

"I know who you are, Doctor. I know all about you. Sherlock's told me a good deal about you." He said it in a knowing tone which I found vaguely disquieting.

"Indeed. And what can I do for you?"

"Well, I think for a start you might have the courtesy to offer me a drink. Yes, a drink. It's devilish cold out there." He said this with the greatest conviction as he sat before me, sweating like a stuck pig.

"What can I give you?"

"Brandy if you have it. I 'most always take a little brandy at this time of the day. It keeps up the strength, you know."

"Very well. Tea is about to be laid on if you prefer."

"Tea?" he gasped. "Tea? Great heavens, Doctor, do you wish to kill me? Being a medical man, I felt sure you knew about tea. The great crippler—that's what tea is. More men my age drop dead as a result of reckless and intemperate consumption of tea than from almost any other single cause save the colic. You were

unaware of that fact, sir? Dear me, where have you
been? Do you read no other pieces in the *Strand*
magazine than your own? Do you honestly suppose
I'd be the living picture of health that I am if I took
tea?"

"Brandy it is, then," said I, suppressing an overpowering impulse to laugh and fetching a glass for
him. Holmes certainly knew the queerest people,
though what his connection with this aged toper was,
I couldn't for the life of me fathom.

I handed him the drink and resumed my chair.
"And what is your message for Mr. Holmes?"

"My message?" The brown eyes clouded. "Oh, yes,
my message! Tell Mr. Holmes—this isn't very good
news, I'm afraid—tell him that his land investments
in Torquay are all wet."

"Wet?"

"Yes, wet, I'm afraid. Dropped into the sea, they
have."

"I was unaware that Mr. Holmes had invested in
land in Torquay."

"Everything he had," the estate agent assured me
gravely, picking up his glass and burying his nose in it.

"What?"

He nodded, shaking his massive head from side to
side in a despairing attitude. "Poor man. For years he's
been instructing me to buy up property overlooking
the sea—seems to have been an idea with him to build
some kind of hotel there—but now, you see, it's all
gone to smash. You've heard about the storm we've
been endurin' there these past four days? No? Well, sir,
I don't mind telling you I've lived in those parts all my
life and never seen anything like it. Plymouth almost
destroyed by floods—and huge chunks of land toppling
right into the channel. The map makers'll have to get
busy, make no mistake." He buried his enormous nose
in the brandy once more as I digested this information.

"And do you mean to tell me that Mr. Holmes's land—all of it?—has been washed into the ocean?"

"Every square inch of it, bless you, sir. He's ruined, Doctor. That's the melancholy errand that brings me up to town."

"Great Scot!" I leapt to my feet in agitation as the full force of the catastrophe made itself felt. "Ruined!" I sank into my chair, stunned by the suddenness of it all.

"You look as though you could do with a drink yourself, Doctor, if you don't mind my saying so."

"I think perhaps I could." I rose on unsteady legs and poured a second brandy while the fellow broke into a low laugh behind me.

"You find this amusing?" I demanded sternly.

"Well, you must admit it *is* rather humourous. A man invests every cent he owns in land—the safest possible investment, you'd say—and then it falls right off into the water. Come now, sir, admit in all honesty that there is a kind of humour to it."

"I fail to see anything of the kind," I returned with heat. "And I find your indifference to your client's plight positively revolting! You come here, drink the man's brandy, calmly report his financial reverses, and then laugh about them!"

"Well, sir, put that way—" The fellow began some clumsy show of remorse, but I was in no mood for it.

"I think you'd better go. I shall break the news to him myself—and in my own way."

"Just as you say, sir," he replied, handing me back the brandy glass. "Though I must confess, I think you're taking a very narrow view of all this. Try to see the humour of it."

"That will do, Mr. Jackson." I turned on my heel and replaced the glass on the sideboard.

"Quite right, Watson," said a familiar voice behind me. "I think it time to ring for tea."

ELEVEN

# Theories
# and Charges

"Holmes!"

I spun 'round and beheld the detective sitting where I had left the estate agent. He was pulling off his huge nose and stripping his head of white hair.

"Holmes, this is monstrous!"

"I'm afraid it was," he agreed, spitting out the wadding he had held in his cheeks to inflate them. "Childish, I positively concur. It was such a good disguise, however, that I had to try it on someone who knew me really well. I could think of no one who fitted that description so conveniently as yourself, my dear fellow."

He stood and removed his coat, revealing endless padding beneath. I sat down, shaking, and watched in silence as he divested himself of his costume and threw on his dressing gown.

"Hot in there," he noted with a smile, "but it worked wonders for me. Still, I'm afraid there are a few loose ends which my new data fail to tie up. By all means, let's have tea."

He rang downstairs, and Mrs. Hudson shortly appeared with the tray, much astonished to find Sherlock

Holmes in residence. "I didn't hear you come in, sir."

"You let me in yourself, Mrs. Hudson."

Her comments at this piece of intelligence are not relevant here. She departed, and Holmes and I pulled up chairs.

"Your eyes!" I cried suddenly, the kettle in my hand. "They're brown!"

"What? Oh, just a minute." He bent forward in his chair, so that he was looking at the floor, and pulled back the skin by his right temple, cupping his other hand beneath his right eye. Into his palm dropped a little brown dot. As I watched, nonplussed, he repeated the operation with his left eye.

"What in the name of all that's wonderful—" I began.

"Behold the ultimate paraphernalia of disguise, Watson." He stretched forth his hand and allowed me to view the little things. "Be careful. They are glass and very delicate."

"But what are they?"

"A refinement of my own—to alter the one feature of a man's face no paint can change. I am not the inventor," he hastened to assure me, "though I venture to say I am the first to apply these little items for this purpose."

"For what purpose are they intended?"

"A very specific one. Some twenty years ago a German in Berlin discovered that he was losing his sight due to an infection on the inside of his eyelids that was spreading to the eyes themselves. He designed a concave piece of glass—rather larger than these and clear, of course—to be inserted between the lid and the cornea, where they were held in place by surface tension. They retarded the disease and saved his sight.*

* Precisely right. Contact lenses are over one hundred years old.

123

I read of his research and modified the design slightly, with the results that you have seen."

"But if the glass should break!" I winced at the thought.

"It isn't likely. Provided you don't rub your eyes, the chances of anything hitting the lenses directly are remote. I use them rarely—they take some getting used to, and I find I cannot wear them for more than a few hours. After that they begin to hurt, and if a speck of dust should enter the eye, I find myself weeping as though at a funeral."

He took the little circles back and placed them in a small box evidently designed to contain them.

"You may be doing yourself an irreparable injury," I warned, feeling obliged, as a medical man, to point out some of the obvious pitfalls to him.

"Von Bülow wore them for twenty years without ill effect. In any event, I consulted your friend Dr. Doyle about them. He is so caught up in his literary whirl that we forget he is also an ophthalmologist. He was extremely helpful in his suggestions for the modifications I had in mind. Zeiss ground them for me," he went on, pocketing the box, "though I fancy they can't have imagined why. Now—" he filled his pipe and held out his teacup—"what of Bernard Shaw?"

Doing my best to adjust to these successive shocks, I poured out the tea and recounted in a few words the tale of my meeting at the Café Royal. Save for asking an occasional pointed question, he heard me out in silence, puffing steadily on his briar and sipping his tea.

"He thought it a practical joke, then?" was his comment regarding Shaw's account of the mysterious assault. "What a whimsical turn of mind he must have."

"I don't feel he thought about it much at all—or

wanted to." I found myself defending the critic. "He was in such a hurry to reach Wilde."

"Hmm. I wonder who else has been pressed to sample this tonic."

"You don't think it a practical joke, then?" I asked, knowing perfectly well that he did not.

He smiled. "Most impractical, wouldn't you say?"

"And what did you discover this afternoon?" I demanded in turn.

He rose and began a perambulation of the room, his hands thrust deep into the pockets of his dressing gown, smoke emanating from his pipe, as from the funnel of a locomotive. He did not appear to notice that I had cleared the floor for him.

"First I paid a visit to Mr. Stoker's clandestine flat in Porkpie Lane," he commenced. "I ascertained (without his knowing it) that he cannot account for his whereabouts during the time of either murder. I learned, as you did, his true Christian name and his former calling as a drama critic. Next I called upon Jessie Rutland's former lodgings (off the Tottenham Court Road) and spoke with the landlady. She was guarded but more helpful than she knew."

"This fits in perfectly with a theory I have been developing all afternoon!" I cried, jumping to my feet. "Would you care to hear it?"

"Certainly. You know I am endlessly fascinated by the workings of your mind." He took the chair I had left.

"Very well. Jessie Rutland meets Bram Stoker. He does not reveal his name or true identity but pretends instead to have recently returned from India, where he has left his invalid wife. He even smokes Indian cigars to bolster this impression. He lets a room in Soho to pursue his intrigue, but somehow Jonathan McCarthy, an old rival from the drama desk who patronises the Savoy, discovers his game and threatens the girl with exposure unless she succumbs to his attentions. Fearing for herself and also for her lover, she agrees. Stoker learns of her sacrifice and contacts McCarthy, who feels free to change his game and ask for money. They agree to a meeting to discuss the price of discretion. During their conversation— which begins leisurely enough, over brandy and cigars —tempers flare, and Stoker, seizing the letter opener, drives it home. He was perfectly capable of this," I added excitedly as more pieces of the puzzle began falling into place pell-mell, "because he was not only athletic champion of Dublin University, but brother to the well-known physician, William Stoker, from whom he had very likely received a cursory but adequate introduction to anatomy. As you yourself have pointed out, he is the right height and wears the right shoes."

"Brilliant, Watson. Brilliant," my companion murmured, relighting his pipe with a warm coal from the fire. "And then?"

"He leaves. McCarthy is still breathing, however, and he forces himself to the bookshelf. The copy of Shakespeare in his hand was meant to indicate the Lyceum, where the specialty is the Bard. Irving is even now producing *Macbeth*. Stoker, in the meantime, has begun to panic. He knows that when Miss Rutland learns of McCarthy's death—as assuredly she must— there will be no doubt in her mind as to the identity of his murderer. The thought of another living soul with his secret begins to gnaw at him like a cancer. What if the police should ever question her? Could she withstand their enquiries? He decides there is only one solution. The Savoy is no great distance from the Lyceum. He slips backstage and leaves the theatre through the Old Beefsteak Club Room, and runs quickly to the Savoy, where he accomplishes the second crime during the rehearsal of *The Grand Duke*, which he knows is in progress. Then he retreats hastily to the Lyceum again, with no-one the wiser. There! What do you think of that?"

For a time he did not respond, but sat puffing at his briar with his eyes closed. Were it not for the continuous stream of smoke, I should have wondered if he was awake. Finally he opened his eyes and withdrew the pipe stem.

"As far as it goes, it is quite brilliant. Really, Watson, I must congratulate you. I marvel, especially, at the many uses to which you have put that volume of *Romeo and Juliet*. Why did McCarthy not choose *Macbeth*, then, if he wished—as you say—to point a finger at the Lyceum?"

"Perhaps he couldn't see by then," I hazarded.

Holmes shook his head with a little smile. "No, no. He saw well enough to turn over the leaves of the volume he selected. That is merely one objection to your theory, despite the fact that there are some really pretty things in it. It appears to explain much, I grant you, but in reality it explains nothing."

"Nothing?"

"Well, almost nothing," he amended, leaning over and tapping me consolingly on the knee. "You mustn't feel offended, my dear chap. I assure you I have no theory whatsoever. At least none that will accommodate your omissions."

"And what are they, I should like to know?"

"Let us take them in order. In the first place, how did Jessie Rutland meet Bram Stoker—so that no one we have questioned knew of it? Male company is severely discouraged at the Savoy, as you know. Where, then? At Miss Rutland's former lodgings that reverend dame, the landlady, spoke quite highly of Miss Rutland and said she had but once seen her boarder in the company of a man—and it was not a man with a beard. She would not be more specific, but that information appears to rule out either of the two men in question. Now, as to friend McCarthy's engagement calendar. Can you see him, in a mood however jocular, referring to Bram Stoker as a love-lorn jester? Is there anything particularly hapless about Stoker, or feeble? Or amusing? I think not. Say, rather, does he not strike the casual observer as menacing, sinister, and quite powerful? And having said that, are you prepared to explain how our Miss Rutland could fall in love with him, any more readily than you reject the idea of her falling in love with the critic? And granting for the moment that she *did* love Stoker and he returned her affection, how are you prepared to explain McCarthy's incautious behaviour in bringing such a man to his own home, where there were no witnesses to ensure his safety? According to your theory, he had seduced the lady and then proposed to extort money from her true love. Was it wise to leave himself alone with a man he had so monstrously wronged? Would he not consider it flying in the face of Providence? Jonathan McCarthy may have been depraved—the evidence suggests it—but there is nothing in the record to support the notion that he was foolhardy."

He paused, knocked the ashes from his pipe, and began to refill it. The action appeared to remind him of something.

"And what of the Indian cigars? Do you seriously contend they were smoked to convince Miss Rutland that Stoker was recently returned from India? I cannot believe her knowledge of tobaccos was sufficient for her to make such fine distinctions. You and I, you may recall, were obliged to visit Dunhill's for a definite identification. For that matter, in the insular world of the theatre, how long could Stoker (if indeed it was he) hope to maintain his Indian deception amongst people who knew him so well? You heard today that his wife is a friend of Gilbert's. How long before Jessie Rutland, working at the Savoy, should stumble upon his true identity? And if, by some odd twist of reasoning, the cigars *were* smoked to contribute to the illusion, why bring them to McCarthy's flat? By your account, the critic knew perfectly well who he was. Indeed, how could he get in touch with him if he didn't? And what about the letter threatening us, its message pasted on Indian stock? Isn't it rather more likely that Jack Point—as I shall continue to call him—is indeed recently returned from India and that this accounts for his choice of tobacco and letter paper? Finally, your theory fails to explain the most singular occurrence in the entire business."

"And what is that?"

"The little matter of the tonics we three were forced to down outside Simpson's last night. Even allowing for Stoker's physical strength and his capacity for *outré* behaviour, what can he have hoped to accomplish by making us drink whatever it was we swallowed? Until we find out, this affair will remain shrouded in mystery."

His logic was so overwhelming that I was reluctantly obliged to succumb. "What will you do now?"

"Smoke. It is quite a three-pipe problem. I am not sure, but it may be more."

With this, he settled himself down amongst a pile of cushions on the floor and proceeded to smoke three additional pipes in rapid succession. He neither moved nor blinked but sat stationary, like the caterpillar in *Alice,* contemplating I knew not what as he polluted our rooms with noxious fumes.

Familiar with this vigil, I occupied my time by trying to read, but even Rider Haggard's fine stories could not engage my attention as the dark settled over London. They seemed tame indeed when compared with the mystery that confronted us—a mystery as tangled and complex as any I could recall in the long and distinguished career of my friend. Holmes had been correct when he spoke of the liquid we had been forced to swallow as the key to the business. Try as I might, however, I could scarcely remember what it tasted like, and my inability to recall anything of the persistent host who served it—save for his gloves—teased me beyond endurance.

Holmes was in the act of filling a fourth pipe—his disreputable clay—when his ritual and my impatience were brought to a simultaneous end by a knock on the door, followed by the entrance of a very cocksure Inspector Lestrade.

"Found any murderers lately, Mr. Holmes?" he demanded with a mischievous air as he removed his coat. The man's idea of subtlety was elephantine.

"Not lately." The detective looked up calmly from the centre of his mushroom-like arrangement of cushions.

"Well, I have," crowed the little man.

"Indeed? The murderer of Jonathan McCarthy?"

"And the murderer of Miss Jessie Rutland. You didn't know these crimes were related, did you? Well, they are—they positively are. Miss Rutland was the mistress of the late critic, and they were both dispatched by the same hand."

"Indeed?" Holmes repeated, turning pale. It would cut him to the quick, I knew, should this fool manage to solve the two murders before himself. His vanity and professional pride were at stake. Everything he stood for in the way of criminal detection demanded that his methods not be beaten by any so haphazard and clumsy as those of Scotland Yard.

"Indeed?" he echoed a third time. "And have you found out why the murderer should smoke Indian cigars?"

"Indian cigars?" Lestrade guffawed. "Are you still

going on about them? Well, if you must know, I'll explain it to you. He smoked them because he's an Indian himself."

"What?" we exclaimed together.

"That's right, a sambo, a Parsee. His name is Achmet Singh, and he's been in England just under a year, running a used-furniture* and curio shop in the Tottenham Court Road with his mother." Lestrade walked about the room, chuckling and rubbing his hands together, scarcely able to contain his self-satisfaction and glee.

If Sherlock Holmes felt chagrinned by the policeman's news, he did his best to conceal the fact. "Where did he meet Miss Rutland?"

"His shop is just down the road from her boarding house. The landlady identified him for me, saying he used to call for her there and take her out walking. The woman was so scandalised by the thought of her lodger taking up with a brown devil that she didn't open up to you about it." He laughed again. "At least I assume it was you she was talking to earlier in the day." He gestured with his hands, delineating a corpulent belly, laughing some more. "That's where being official police comes in handy, Mr. Holmes."

"May I ask what he was doing with tobacco if he is a Parsee?"

" 'What's he doing in England?' You might as well ask! But if he came here to mingle with white folk, he'll 'ave taken to some of our ways, no doubt. Why, the fellow was even attending evening classes at the University of London."

"Ah. A sure sign of a criminal mind."

"You can jeer," the inspector returned, undisturbed. "The point is—" he placed a forefinger emphatically

---

* "Used furniture" and "second-hand furniture" are accepted British synonyms for our American "antiques."

on the detective's chest—"the point is that the man cannot account for his time during the period when either murder took place. He had the time and the motive," the policeman concluded triumphantly.

"The motive?" I interjected.

"Jealousy! Heathen passion! You can see that, surely, Doctor. She dropped him and took up with that newspaper chap—"

"Who invited him to his home, where the Parsee drank brandy," Holmes offered mildly.

"Who knows if he drank a drop? The glass was knocked on its side with the drink still in it. He might have accepted the offer of a glass simply as part of his plan to gain admittance to the place."

"He went there, of course, knowing a murder weapon of some sort was bound to be ready to hand—"

"I didn't say the plan was murder," Lestrade countered. "I didn't say anything about premeditated murder, did I? He may simply have wanted to plead for the return of his white woman." Lestrade stood up and took his coat. "He's almost the right height. He's right-handed, too."

"And his shoes?"

Lestrade grinned broadly. "His shoes, Mr. Holmes, are three weeks old and were purchased in the Strand."

# TWELVE

# The Parsee and
# Porkpie Lane

After Lestrade had gone, Sherlock Holmes sat motionless for a considerable period of time. He looked to be in such a brown study that I did not like to disturb him, but my own anxiety was so great that I was unable to remain silent for very long.

"Hadn't we best speak with the man?" I asked, throwing myself into a chair before him. He looked up at me slowly, his countenance creased with thought.

"I suppose we had," he allowed, getting to his feet and assembling his clothes. "It is as well in such circumstances to go through the motions."

"Do you think, then, that they can have apprehended the guilty party?"

"The guilty party?" He considered the question, thrusting some keys into his waistcoat pocket and taking a bull's-eye lantern from behind the deal table. "I doubt it. There are too many explanations, and phrases such as 'almost the right height' give away the holes in their case. However, we'd best take a look, if only to find out what didn't happen." He came forward with the gravest expression I had ever beheld on his face. "I have an inkling about this that bodes ill, Watson. Lestrade has built up a neat circumstantial case in which the hideous spectre of racial bigotry plays a large and unsubtle rôle. Achmet Singh may not be guilty, but the odds are against him."

He said no more on the subject but allowed me to ponder his view of the situation during a silent cab drive to Whitehall. There was no great difficulty in our being admitted to interview the prisoner, Lestrade's visit having included an invitation to see the man for ourselves.

The moment we were shown to Singh's cell, Sherlock Holmes breathed a sigh of relief. The man we studied through the small window of his cell door was diminutive in stature and wiry of build. He appeared neither large enough nor strong enough to perform the physical feats counsel would have to attribute to him. Moreover, he wore a pair of the thickest spectacles I had ever seen and was reading a newspaper held only an inch or so from his nose.

Holmes nodded to the guard, who unlocked the door.

"Achmet Singh?"

"Yes?" A pair of dark brown eyes squinted up at us from behind the glasses. "Who is that?"

"I am Sherlock Holmes. This is Dr. Watson."

"Sherlock Holmes!" The little fellow came forward eagerly. "Dr. Watson!" He made to seize our hands but thought better of it and drew back, suspiciously. "What do you want?"

"To help you if we can," said Holmes kindly. "May we sit down?"

Singh shrugged and vaguely indicated his meagre pallet. "There is no help for me," he responded in a trembling voice. "I cannot account for my time, and I knew the girl. Also, my shoes are the right size and purchased in the wrong place. Finally, I am coloured. What jury in the world could resist such a combination?"

"A British jury will resist it," I said, "provided we can show that the prosecution cannot prove its case."

"Bravo, Watson!" Holmes sat down on the cot and motioned for me to do the same. "Mr. Singh, why don't you tell us your version of events? Cigarette?" He made as if to reach for a case in his pocket, but the other declined it with a distracted wave of his hand.

"My religion denies me the consolations of tobacco and liquor."

"What a pity." Holmes could scarcely conceal a smirk. "Now tell me what you know of this business."

"What can I tell you, since I did not kill poor Miss Rutland and do not know who did?" Tears stood in the miserable wretch's eyes, magnified pathetically by his thick lenses, which almost seemed to double his sorrow.

"You must tell us what you can, however unimportant it may seem to you. Let us begin with Miss Rutland. How did you come to know her?"

The prisoner leaned up against the brick wall next to the door and directed his voice to the corner: "She came into my shop, which is just 'round the corner from her room. I deal in curios from the East, as well as second-hand English furniture, and she liked to look at the things there when she had some time to herself. I would answer her questions about the pieces she liked and tell her what I could of their origins. Slowly we began to discuss other matters. She was an orphan, and my mother had passed away not long before. Aside from my customers and her friends in the theatre, we neither of us knew many people." He paused and swallowed painfully, his Adam's apple protruding from the tightened muscles in his scrawny neck, as he turned and faced the detective across the cell. "We were lonely, Mr. Holmes. Is that a crime?"

"Indeed, it is not," said my companion gently. "Go on."

"Then we began to go for walks. Nothing more, I give you my word!" he added hastily. "Only walks. In the evening before the weather turned cold and she had to leave for the theatre, we strolled. And we continued our conversations."

"I understand."

"Do you?" He emitted a laugh that resembled nothing so much as a sob. "That is good. Inspector Lestrade does not. He places a rather different construction on my behaviour."

"Do not concern yourself with Inspector Lestrade for the moment. Pray continue your narrative."

"There isn't any more. Wherever we walked, people stared at us and whispered as we passed. At first we paid no attention. We were so lonely, our loneliness lent us the courage to defy conventions."

"And then?"

He sighed and his shoulders shook. "And then we began to notice. It frightened us. We tried to ignore our fears for a time, but we were too frightened even to mention them to one another. And then—" He hesitated, confused by his own recollections.

"Yes?"

"She met another man." His low voice made it difficult to catch the words. "A white man. It pained her to tell me," he continued, tears rolling freely down his cheeks now, "but our awkwardness together increased. Our fears grew greater. There were little incidents—a word overheard as we walked by a knot of tradesmen—and she became more terrified and reluctant to go with me when I came to call for her. Still, she did not know how to tell me of her fears or of the man she had met. I do not think she wished to tell me." He paused. "So I told her. I said our being seen together so frequently was beginning to excite

comment in the neighbourhood and I thought it better
that such talk be stopped lest it injure her reputation
or get back to the theatre. She tried not to show her
relief when I said these things, but I could see a great
weight had been lifted from her shoulders. She was a
good person, Mr. Holmes, kind and generous to a
fault, and it was not her way to abandon a friend. It
was then that she told me about the man she had met.
The white man," he repeated in a tone so helpless that
it wrenched my heart to listen to it.

"What did she say about him?"

"Why, nothing but that she had met him and come
to love him. The rules at the Savoy are terribly strict
regarding such things, and she was forced to be discreet. Also, I think she did not wish to pain me with
the details. That is why we never ventured into other
neighbourhoods than our own," he added. "Because
it would have meant ruin for her at the theatre had
she been recognised in my company." He looked up at
us from the kneeling posture to which he had succumbed. "That is all there is to tell."

"What are you studying at the university?"

"Law."

"I see." Holmes went over and shook his hand. "Mr.
Singh, I beg of you to be of good cheer. The matter
stands against you for the time being, but I shall see
to it that you never appear in the dock."

For some moments the Indian studied him search-
ingly from behind his thick spectacles. "Why should
it matter to you whether I stand there or not? I do
not know you and cannot possibly pay you for any
trouble you take on my behalf."

Sherlock Holmes's grey eyes grew moist with an
emotion I had seldom seen there. "To pursue the truth
in this world is a trouble we should all undertake
gladly on our own behalf," said he.

The Parsee looked at him, swallowing and unable to speak, the tears still streaming down his face.

"The man's vision is hopelessly astigmatic," Holmes observed as we emerged from the gloomy building. "Did you notice how he was forced to read his paper?" My friend's customary detachment of voice and facial expression had been forcibly restored. "To imagine that he can even see clearly across a table the size of the one in McCarthy's flat is as difficult as it is to envisage someone of his size striking a single fatal blow from that distance with a blunt-tipped letter opener."

"What do you propose, then?"

He looked at his watch in the light of the street lamp. "A little past eight," he noted. "The theatres are busy. Would you care to accompany me on an excursion, Doctor?"

"An excursion? Where?"

"Number Fourteen Porkpie Lane, Soho."

"To Bram Stoker's flat?"

"Yes."

"We are going to burgle it?"

"If you've no objection."

"None whatever. But why, if you reject my theory, does the place interest you?"

"We have no choice in view of recent developments—" he gestured with a crooked thumb in the general direction of the jail—"but to eliminate even the outside suspects in this matter. I can emerge with no theory of my own, and Stoker taunts us like an apparition. Perhaps we can exorcise his influence on our thinking. For this purpose I have brought a bull's-eye and some keys which may be useful to us. Are you coming? Good. Cab!"

The cab took us into a part of the West End with which I was not familiar. We threaded our way at first through well, if garishly lit neighbourhoods, listening

to raucous laughter and tinny music, and then passed
into an area where even the occasional street lamp
provided scant illumination. Looking about in the
gloom, I felt little inclined to remain in one place and
did not like the thought of being stranded there. Not
many folk were about in this quarter of the town; at
any rate, not many were visible, but I sensed them
behind windows, around corners, and in the menacing
shadows of buildings. Our cab was obviously a novelty
in the vicinity, a distinction keenly felt by the driver,
whom I could hear muttering an unceasing string of
maledictions above us. The horse's hooves echoed
eerily on the deserted cobblestones.

Number 14 Porkpie Lane was a three-storey affair
which looked positively squeezed between its neighbours, two seedy constructions on either side of it.
Somewhat taller, they leaned towards one another
over the roof of number 14, creating a vise-like impression.

"Which is it?" I asked, looking up at the queer
structure.

"On the second storey, in the middle. The window's
dark, as you can see. It has a little ledge beneath it."

"Someone thought of putting a balcony there once."

"Very likely."

We descended from the cab and made arrangements with the unwilling driver to come back in an
hour and fetch us home. He was not loath to go, and
I could not blame him, for the setting was not in any
way appealing. I only hoped he would prove as good
as his word and return.

We waited in the shadows of the nearest edifice
until the horse had clattered 'round the corner. Then,
looking carefully about, Holmes produced a latchkey
from his pocket and held it up to the faint light.

"A very useful item, this," said he softly. "I had it
from Tony O'Hara, the sneak thief, when I nabbed

him. You recall the case, Watson? It was a sort of parting gift, an entire ring of these little beauties. Each will tackle a great many simple locks of the same make. If one fails, you have only to move 'round the ring."

"You chose only two this night," I pointed out as he inserted the key in the front door lock and began to fiddle and twist with it. "How did you know which to bring?"

"By examining the locks this afternoon."

"I had no idea you were so adept at breaking and entering."

"Quite adept," he replied cheerfully, "and always ready in a good cause. It is always the cause that justifies little felonies such as these." His eyes twinkled in the dark. "*L'homme c'est rien, l'oeuvre c'est tout*. Come along, Watson."

The lock had yielded to his gentle ministrations, and now the door opened before us, the small passage on the other side of it leading instantly to a rickety flight of stairs. We ascended without hesitation, judging that the less time we spent exposed to view, the safer we should be. I looked about as we climbed, wondering what sort of place it was.

A step or two behind me on the stair, the detective read my thoughts. "It's a sort of boarding house of the kind that caters to transient characters," he informed me. "Keep moving."

It took rather more time to open the door to the flat, but after some delicate manipulations, this obstacle was also overcome and we found ourselves in the private sanctuary of Bram Stoker.

Holmes opened the bull's-eye, and we surveyed the small room.

"Not suffused with romance," he commented drily, holding the lantern high above his head and turning slowly. The room, though shabby, was nonetheless neat and spare. There were only three articles of furniture to be seen: a desk, a chair, and small day bed. On the desk was a lone inkwell and a blotter. The cracked and peeling walls boasted not a single picture nor decoration of any sort.

"Scarcely a trysting place," I agreed, looking at Holmes.

He grunted by way of reply and moved towards the desk. "I begin to see the logic of it, Watson. Our Mr. Stoker's secret mistress is the muse of literature. But why all the circumspection?" He sat down before the desk, setting the lantern on top of it, and began pulling open drawers. I advanced behind him and looked over his shoulder as he drew forth bundles of paper covered with small, neat, surprisingly feminine handwriting.

"Have a look at some of this." He passed me a sheaf, and I began to read, standing next to him for want of a chair or other source of light. The man had apparently copied out a series of letters, extracts from diaries and personal notes written or exchanged among people named Jonathan Harker, Lucy Westenra, Dr. Abraham Van Helsing, Arthur Holmwood, and Mina Murray.

"This must be some sort of novel," Holmes intoned softly, bent over a portion of it.

"A novel? Surely not."

"Yes, a novel, written in the form of letters and journals. Does nothing strike you about the name Jonathan Harker?"

"I suppose it vaguely resembles Stoker's real name."

"Vaguely? It contains precisely the number of syllables, and they are distributed between Christian and surnames in exactly the same manner. Stoker and Harker are almost identical, and Jonathan and Abraham are culled from the same source, the Bible. Harker must be his literary self."

"Why, then, is there a Doctor *Abraham* Van Helsing?" I asked, showing him the name. He read it, frowning.

"Name games, name games," he murmured. "Obviously that part of my assumption was incorrect—or at any rate incomplete." He continued reading, turning over the pages of the manuscript in an orderly fashion, his lips pursed with concentration.

"Look at this," he said after the space of a few minutes' silence. I returned from an idle tour of the room and read over his shoulder again:

On the bed beside the window lay Jonathan Harker, his face flushed and breathing heavily, as though in a stupor. Kneeling on the edge of the bed, facing outwards, was the white-clad figure of his wife; by her side stood a tall, thin man, the Count. His right hand gripped the back of her neck, forcing her face down on his bosom. Her white nightdress was smeared with blood, and a thin stream trickled down the man's bare chest, which was shown by his torn, open dress. The attitude of the two had a terrible resemblance to a child forcing a kitten's nose into a saucer of milk to compel it to drink.*

"Great heavens!" I exclaimed, looking up and passing a hand before my eyes. "This is depraved."

"And this." He set down another passage before me:

* This passage and the characters' names make it abundantly plain that the manuscript in question was an early draft of *Dracula*, begun in 1895 by Stoker and published in 1897. Ellen Terry's mention of "when it happened the first time" undoubtedly refers to the publication of Stoker's short stories, *Under the Sunset*. Henry Irving was extremely possessive about Stoker's time.

". . . and you are now to me, flesh of my flesh, blood of my blood, kin of my kin; my bountiful wine press for a while." He then pulled open the shirt with his long, sharp nails, and opened a vein in his breast. When the blood began to spurt out, he took my hands in one of his, holding them tight, and with the other seized my neck and pressed my mouth to the wound, so that I might either suffocate or swallow some of the—oh, my God, what have I done?

"Holmes, what sort of mad work is this?"

"No wonder he writes in secrecy," the detective remarked, looking up. "Have you noticed anything else?"

"What do you mean?"

"Only that our Mr. Stoker knows how to induce swallowing." I looked at the two passages again, and we stared at each other, horror written on our faces.

"Can we have been forced to drink blood?" I whispered in awed tones.

Before he could answer, we were both made aware of the clip-clop of horse's hooves entering the lane.

"The cab's not due back yet," Holmes observed, snapping shut the bull's-eye and plunging the room into darkness. He peered through the shutters into the street. "Great Scott! It's *he*!"

"The cabbie?"

"Stoker!"

# THIRTEEN

# The Missing
# Policeman

"Hurry, Watson." Rapidly Holmes assembled the papers and replaced them in the drawers from which he had taken them. As we heard the cab door slam in the stillness, he lept to the door of the flat and locked it from within.

"But, Holmes—"

"The balcony, man! Quick!"

In less time than it takes to report, we threw open the window and passed out on to the precarious ledge, closing the shutters behind us as Stoker's heavy tread became audible on the stair.

"Don't look down," were my companion's last instructions as we flattened ourselves against the building wall and awaited further developments.

We had not long to wait. Within seconds of our gaining tenuous positions of safety, the door to the flat was reopened and Stoker entered the room. He closed and locked the door behind him, then proceeded to his desk, lit the gas, and pulled open the drawers. He took out pens, fresh paper, and what he had already written, spent some minutes ordering his materials, but did not appear to notice anything amiss. Without further preamble he settled down to work on his ghastly manuscript.

How long we stood on that slender shelf, clutching the bottom of the window frame for support, it is difficult to say. The moon had risen, pinning us like specimens beneath an observation light. We dared not move, for we were so near the clandestine novelist that our merest sound was certain to excite his suspicions. As the time passed and we prayed for the return of our cab, our hands, even in their gloves, began to lose sensation. The stillness around us was broken only by an occasional cough from within.

After what seemed a year, the silence was abruptly shattered by the hoofbeats of another horse. Holmes and I exchanged looks, and he signed for me to peer under the shutters. I did so and was able to discern the bending author in pursuit of his story, happily indifferent to any disturbance outside his mad world. I looked again at Holmes, indicating with a blink of my eyes that all was well, and he gestured with a free hand, explaining that we must jump on to the roof of the cab as it stopped underneath.

The poor cabby entered the alley nervously and looked about. Holmes signalled from our perch above and waved him over, placing a finger on his lips in a theatrical plea for silence. The man appeared quite dumbfounded by the sight of us hanging, as it were, from the moon but responded to the detective's repeated gesticulations and moved the vehicle hesitantly forward. When he had arranged the cab's position perfectly, we lowered ourselves gingerly to the roof before him, making but little noise in the process.

When we had landed, Holmes clapped the cabby on the back in a grateful embrace. "Baker Street," he urged quietly, and we returned to our lodgings, leaving the fiendish Mr. Stoker to his queer literary efforts.

"Your theory has had another hole punched in it," Holmes remarked as we climbed the seventeen steps to our rooms. "Bram Stoker's secret lair is used for his writing, not his rendezvous, given that his pastime is one of which his family and employer disapprove."

"I can see why," I acknowledged. "But what about the passages in the book—the ones in which folk are compelled to drink—?"

"I was thinking about them on our way back," he returned, stopping on the stair. "You will find that if you wish to induce swallowing, there is only one way to go about it. No, Watson, I am afraid matters have come to a very serious pass. We might wish Bram Stoker to be our man, but he is not—no more than is that miserable wretch Lestrade has arrested. The only difference between them," he added, opening the door, "is that if we cannot find the true murderer, Achmet Singh will hang. Hullo! Who is here? Why, it's young Hopkins!"

It was indeed the sandy-haired policeman, who was just being shown to a chair by our landlady as we entered. He rose awkwardly at once and explained that Mrs. Hudson had told him he might wait for us there.

"Quite right, Mrs. Hudson," Holmes assured her, interrupting her flow of oratory on the subject. "I know that you don't like policemen standing about in your parlour."

The long-suffering woman referred briefly to the strange goings-on of late (by which she meant, I knew, Holmes's appearance in disguise that afternoon) and withdrew.

"Now, then, Hopkins," Holmes began as soon as the door had closed, "what brings you to Baker Street at an hour when most off-duty policemen are at home, resting their feet? I perceive that your route here has been a circuitous one and that you have taken great pains to avoid being seen."

"Heavens, sir, how can you tell that?"

"My dear young man, you have divested yourself of every vestige of your police uniform, which means you probably stopped at home first. And then, look at your trouser leg. There must be seven different splashes there, each evidently from a different part of town. I believe I recognise some mud from Gloucester Road, the cement they are using at the Kensington—"

"I have had to be extremely circumspect." The youth blushed and looked uncertainly from one to the other of us.

"You may speak before Dr. Watson here as before myself," Holmes promised smoothly.

"Very well." He sighed and took what was palpably a difficult plunge. "I must tell you gentlemen straight off that my appearance here tonight puts me in a very awkward situation—with the force, I mean." He eyed us anxiously. "I've come on my own initiative, you see, and not in any official capacity."

"Bravo," Holmes murmured. "I was right, Hopkins. There is hope for you."

"I very much doubt if there will be at the Yard if they learn of this," the forlorn policeman replied, his honest features clouding further at the thought. "Perhaps I'd best be—"

"Why don't you pull that chair up to the fire and begin at the beginning?" Holmes interrupted with soothing courtesy. "There you are. Make yourself quite at home and comfortable. Would you care for something to drink? No? Very well, I am all attention." To prove it, he crossed his legs and closed his eyes.

"It's about Mr. Brownlow," the sergeant commenced hesitantly. He saw that Holmes's eyes were shut and looked at me, perplexed, but I motioned for him to go on. "Mr. Brownlow," he repeated. "You know Mr. Brownlow?"

"The police surgeon? I believe I passed him on my

way downstairs at Twenty-four South Crescent yesterday morning. He was on his way for McCarthy's remains, was he not?"

"Yes, sir." Hopkins ran a tongue over his dry lips.

"A good man, Brownlow. Did he find anything remarkable in his autopsy?"

There was a pause.

"Did he?"

"We don't know, Mr. Holmes."

"But he's submitted his report, surely."

"No. The fact is—" Hopkins hesitated again—"Mr. Brownlow has disappeared."

Holmes opened his eyes. "Disappeared?"

"Yes, Mr. Holmes. He's quite vanished."

The detective blew air soundlessly from his cheeks. With automatic gestures his slender hands began nervously packing a pipe which had been lying near to hand. "When was he last seen?"

"He was in the mortuary all day at work on McCarthy—in the laboratory—and he began acting very strangely."

"How do you mean strangely?"

The sergeant made a funny face, as though about to laugh. "He threw all the assistants and stretcherbearers out of the laboratory; made all of 'em take off all their clothes and scrub down with carbolic and alcohol and shower. And you know what he did while they were showering?"

The detective shook his head. I found myself straining to catch the sergeant's low tones.

"Mr. Holmes, *he burned all their clothes.*"

My companion's eyes grew very bright at this. "Did he, indeed? And then disappeared?"

"Not just yet. He continued to work on the corpse by himself, and then, as you know, Miss Rutland's remains were carried in and he went briefly to work on them. He grew excited all over again and again summoned the stretcher-bearers and his assistants together and made them take off all their clothes once more, scrub with carbolic and alcohol, and shower." He paused, licked his lips and took a breath. "And while they were showering—"

"He burned their clothes a second time?" Holmes enquired. He could not suppress his excitement, and he rubbed his hands together with satisfaction, puffing rapidly on his pipe. The young man nodded.

"It was almost funny. They thought he'd started to play some sort of prank on them the first time, but now they were furious, especially the bearers. They all had to be wrapped in blankets from the emergency room and in the meantime, Mr. Brownlow'd barricaded himself inside the laboratory! They brought Inspector Gregson down from Whitehall, but Mr. Brownlow wouldn't open the door to him, either. He had a police revolver with him in there and threatened to shoot the first man across the threshold. The door is quite solid and has no window, so they were obliged to leave him there all afternoon and into the night."

"And now?"

"Now he is gone."

"Gone? How? Surely they had sense enough to post a man outside the laboratory door."

Hopkins nodded vigorously. "They did, but they didn't think to post one outside the back of the laboratory."

"And where does that door lead?"

"To the stables and mews. The laboratory receives its supplies that way. The door is bigger and easier to lock, so that they never thought to challenge it. You see, Mr. Holmes, it never occurred to any of us that his object was to *leave* the laboratory. Quite the reverse. We assumed his purpose was to make us leave, and remain in sole possession. Besides, they could hear him talking to himself in there."

Holmes closed his eyes and leaned back once more in his chair.

"So he left the back way?"

"Ay, sir. In a police van."

"Have you checked at his home? Brownlow's married, I seem to recall, and lives in Knightsbridge. Have you tried him there?"

"He's not been home, sir. We've men posted by it, and neither they nor his Missus have seen hide nor hair. She's quite worked up about it, needless to say."

"How very curious. I take it none of this activity at the mortuary has had the slightest effect on the consensus at the Yard that Achmet Singh is guilty of a double murder?"

"No effect whatsoever, sir, though I venture to suppose there must be a connection of some sort."

"What makes you suppose that?"

Young Hopkins swallowed with difficulty. "Because there's one other thing I haven't told you, Mr. Holmes."

"And that is?"

"Mr. Brownlow took the bodies with him."

Holmes sat forward so abruptly that the sergeant flinched.

"What? Miss Rutland and McCarthy?"

"That is correct, sir." The detective rose and began pacing about the room as the other watched. "I came to you, sir, because in my limited experience, you appear to think much more logically about certain matters than—" he trailed off, embarrassed by his own indiscretion, but Holmes, deep in thought, appeared not to notice.

"Hopkins, would our going over to the laboratory and having a close look at things there place you in an awkward position?"

The young man paled. "Please, sir, you mustn't think of doing it. The fact is, they're all of a dither down there and don't want anyone to know what's happened. They've got it in their heads this thing could make them a laughing stock—the idea of the police surgeon burning all those clothes and then absconding with two corpses. . . ."

"That is one way of looking at it," Holmes agreed. "Very well, then. You must answer a few more questions to the very best of your ability."

"I'll try, sir."

"Have you seen the laboratory since Brownlow abandoned it?"

"Yes, sir. I made it my business to have a look."

"Capital! Really, Hopkins, you exceed my fondest hopes. Now tell me what was left there?"

The sergeant frowned in concentration, eager to continue earning the detective's effusive praise. "Nothing much, I'm afraid. Rather less than usual, in fact. The place had been scrubbed clean as a whistle and it fairly reeked of carbolic. The only thing out of the ordinary was the pile of burnt clothes in the chemical basins where he'd set fire to them. And he'd poured lye over the ashes."

"How did you know what they were, in that case?"

"Some of the buttons still remained, sir."

"Hopkins, you are a trump." Holmes rubbed his hands together once more. "And have your sore throat and headache quite vanished?"

"Quite, sir. Yesterday Lestrade said it was probably just—" He stopped and gaped at the detective. "I don't recall mentioning my illness."

"Nor did you—which doesn't alter the fact of your recovery. I am delighted to learn of it. You haven't left out anything? A little nip of something on the side?"

Hopkins looked at him uncertainly. "Nip? No, sir. I don't know what you mean, I'm afraid."

"Doubtless not. Lestrade feels fit, too, now, does he?"

"He is quite recovered," the sergeant answered, giving up all hope of learning the detective's secrets. Holmes scowled and cupped his chin in thought.

"You are both luckier than you know."

"See here, Holmes," I broke in, "I seem to see what you are getting at. There's some matter of contamination or contagion involved—"

"Precisely." His eyes gleamed. "But we have yet to discover what is in danger of proliferating. Watson, you saw both bodies and conducted a cursory examination of each. Did their condition suggest anything in the nature of a disease to you?"

I sat and pondered while they watched, Holmes barely able to conceal his impatience.

"I believe I stated at the time that both the throats were prematurely stiff, as though the glands were swollen. But any number of common ailments begin with a sore throat."

Holmes sighed, nodded, and turned once more to the policeman. "Hopkins, I very much fear a discreet visit to the back of the mortuary laboratory is inevitable. The stakes are too great that we should hesitate to trifle with the dignity of the metropolitan police. We must see how one man carried out two corpses. We already begin to know why."

"To dispose of them?" I asked.

He nodded grimly. "And it would be as well to put out a general alarm for that missing police van."

"That has already been done, Mr. Holmes," said the young sergeant with some satisfaction. "If it's in London, we'll lay hands on it."

"That is exactly what you must none of you do," Holmes returned, throwing on his coat. "No one must go near it. Watson, are you still game?"

# FOURTEEN

# The West
# End Hororr

Moments later we stood in the company of the anxious sergeant on the stretch of pavement before 221b, in search of a cab. Instead of a hansom, however, I beheld a familiar figure dancing down the street towards us in the glare of the lamplight.

"Have you heard the latest outrage?" Bernard Shaw cried without so much as shaking hands. "They've pinned the whole thing on a Parsee!"

Sherlock Holmes endeavoured to inform the volatile Irishman that we were aware of the turn events had taken, but at that moment Shaw recognised Hopkins and turned upon that unfortunate young man the full force of his sarcastic vitriol.

"Out of uniform, eh?" he commenced. "And well you should be if murder is being contemplated. I wonder you've the face to appear in public at all with your hands so red! Do you seriously believe, Sergeant, that the British public, which I agree is gullible beyond credence, is going to swallow this particular connivance? It won't go down, believe me, Sergeant, it won't. It's too big to pass the widest chasm of plausibility.

This isn't France, you'd do well to remember.* You can't divert *our* attention with a xenophobic charade!"

In vain, as we waited for our cab, did Hopkins attempt to stem the tidal wave of rhetoric. He pointed out that it was not he who had arrested the Indian.

"So!" the other eagerly seized the opportunity for a literary analogy. "You wash your hands with Pilate, hey? I wonder there's room at the trough for so many of you, lined up alongside with your dirty fingers. If you suppose—"

"My dear Shaw," Holmes remonstrated forcefully, "I don't know how you can have learned of Mr. Singh's arrest—the newsboys are hawking it, very likely—but if you have nothing better to do than rouse mine honest neighbours at a quarter past twelve, I suggest you come along with us. Cabby!"

"Where to?" Shaw demanded as the cab pulled up before us. His voice lacked any trace of contrition.

"The mortuary. Someone appears to have made off with our two corpses."

"Made off with them?" he echoed, getting in. This intelligence succeeded in doing what Sergeant Hopkins could not, and the critic fell silent as he tried to determine its significance. His shrill imprecations were reduced to a stream of mutterings as we threaded our way to the mews behind the mortuary laboratory. A street or so before the place, Holmes ordered the driver to stop and we descended from the cab. In hushed tones, the cabby was instructed to wait where he was until we should return.

There was no one about as we entered the mews, though the voices of the ostlers were audible from the police stables across the way. We proceeded cautiously on foot, our path being lit by the yellow lights

* We have no way of knowing what precisely was meant by this remark. In my opinion it refers to the trial of Captain Dreyfus.

of windows overhead. Sergeant Hopkins looked fearfully about as we advanced, being more apprehensive about discovery than ourselves, for obvious reasons.

"This door leads to the laboratory?" Holmes enquired softly, pointing to a large, wooden, portcullislike affair, whose base was some four feet off the ground.

Hopkins nodded, stealing an anxious glance over his shoulder. "That's it, Mr. Holmes."

"You can see the wheel marks where the wagon was backed up to it." The detective knelt and indicated the twin tracks, plainly visible in the meagre light from above. "Of course the police have examined it," he added with a weary sigh, pointing to all the footprints running in every direction all 'round the place.

"It looks like they danced a Highland fling here," I commented, sharing his indignation.

He grunted and followed the wheel marks out of the dirt to where they disappeared on the cobblestones. "He went left; that's all we can say," he reported gloomily, returning to the door where we waited. "Once he departed the mews there's no telling where he was bound."

"Perhaps we should fetch Toby," I suggested.

"We haven't the time to get to Lambeth and back, and besides, what could we offer him as a scent? He's not as young as he used to be, you know, and the stench of carbolic would be insufficient. Blast! Every second gives this thing—whatever it is—more time to spread. Hullo, what's this?"

He had been speaking bent over and almost touching the ground as he inspected it inch by inch. Now he dropped to his knees once again, directly beneath the laboratory door, and rose with something held gingerly in his right hand. "The noose around Achmet Singh's neck begins to loosen, or I am much deceived."

"How so?" Shaw enquired, stepping forward.

"Because if the prosecution contends that the Parsee smoked these Indian cheroots, they will be hard put to explain the presence of this one outside the mortuary whilst Singh himself is incarcerated in a private security cell at Whitehall."

"Are you certain it is the same cigar?" I hazarded, not wishing to question his abilities and yet, for the sake of the prisoner, feeling obliged to do so.

"Quite sure," he returned without seeming to take umbrage. "I took great pains to recognise it should I ever see one like it again. It's in an excellent state of preservation, as you can see. Notice the distinctive square-tipped ends. Our man simply threw it aside when the other opened the laboratory door for him."

"The other?"

Holmes turned to Hopkins. "I take it Mr. Brownlow did not smoke Indian cheroots?"

"No, sir," the youth replied. "In fact, to my knowledge, he did not smoke at all."

"Excellent. Then there was another man here, and it is that other man who concerns us. Brownlow was not talking to himself but conversing with our quarry."

"But what of Mr. Brownlow?" Hopkins demanded, his honest features revealing his perplexity.

"Hopkins—" the detective put a hand upon his shoulder—"the time has come for us to part company. Your position here becomes increasingly delicate as this night progresses. If you will be guided by me, I suggest that for your own good you go home and get a good night's rest. Say nothing to anyone of what you have seen and heard here tonight, and I, for my part, will endeavour to keep your name out of it—unless, of course, Achmet Singh comes to the foot of the gallows, at which point I will have no alternative but to take drastic steps."

Hopkins wavered, torn between his own curiosity

and his sense of discretion. "Will you tell me what you find, at least?" he implored.

"I am afraid I cannot promise that I shall."

The sergeant hesitated a moment or so longer and then departed with evident reluctance, his personal impulses outweighed by the obligations of loyalty he felt he owed to his superiors.

"A bright young fellow, that," Holmes observed when he had gone. "And now, Watson, every minute counts. Whom do you know who could tell us about tropical diseases?"

"Tropical diseases?" Shaw interjected, but Holmes waved him to silence and waited for my answer.

"Ainstree* is generally regarded as the greatest living authority on the subject," I replied, "but he is in the West Indies at present, if I am not mistaken."

"What have tropical diseases to do with this?" Shaw demanded, raising his voice.

"Let us return to the cab, and I will explain. Only keep your voice down, like a good fellow.

"I think we had best pay a call on Dr. Moore Agar, of Harley Street," he resumed when we had regained the cab. "Watson, you've frequently recommended him when I've been suffering from overwork and fatigue."

"I did not envisage your calling upon him after one in the morning," I hastened to point out. "In any case, the man's not a specialist in tropical diseases."

"No, but he may be able to direct us to the leading available authority."

"In heaven's name," Shaw exploded as the cab rattled off for Harley Street, "you still haven't said why we need a specialist in tropical diseases!"

"Forgive me, but I hope to make all plain before

---

* Watson had urged Holmes to consult Ainstree in his capacity as tropical disease expert in *The Adventure of the Dying Detective* (1887).

the night is out. All I can say at present is that Jonathan McCarthy and Miss Jessie Rutland were not killed to prevent their living but rather to prevent their dying a more horrible and more dangerous death."

"How can one death be more dangerous than another?" Shaw scoffed in the dark recesses of the cab.

"Very easily. Different kinds of death pose different hazards to those who continue living. All bodies become sources of infection if they are not disposed of, yet a body that dies a natural death or even one that has been stabbed is less dangerous to other people than a corpse that has succumbed to some virulent disease."

"You mean these two were slain violently in order to prevent their suffering the ravages of some malady?" Shaw exclaimed.

"Just so. A virulent disease that would have made off with them as surely as a bullet, given time. Their corpses were stolen from the mortuary laboratory to prevent further contagion, and we three, who were most prominently exposed to them, were forced to imbibe some sort of antidote."

"Antidote!" the critic cried out, his voice rising an involuntary octave. "Then that practical joke outside Simpson's—"

"Saved our lives, I shouldn't wonder."

"If your theory is correct," Shaw returned gruffly. "But what is the malady we are speaking of?"

"I have no idea and hesitate even to venture a guess. Since all the evidence points to someone recently returned from India, I take the liberty of postulating some tropical disorder, but that is the best I can do with such insufficient data.

"The bodies were no doubt stolen, also, to prevent an autopsy from revealing what would have killed them had the murderer permitted them to live."

"What of Brownlow, then? Did he collaborate with Jack Point?"

"He opened the door to him, that much seems certain. The evidence suggests he had come upon the truth—why else scrub down the laboratory, force the stretcher-bearers to shower, and burn their clothes?"

"Where is he now, then?"

Holmes hesitated. "I very much fear that Mr. Brownlow is dead. If the murderer's purpose was to contain a spreading epidemic, the police surgeon, by virtue of his occupation, was more exposed to contamination than any of us."

Next to me I could see Holmes's jaw tighten, and in his expression I beheld that which I had never seen before in all the years I had known him. I beheld fear.

It was almost two o'clock when the cab deposited us before Dr. Moore Agar's imposing residence in Harley Street. Remarking that our intrusion was not likely to be rendered less irritating to Dr. Agar by our waiting, Holmes proceeded up the steps and rang the night bell vigourously several times. It took some moments before a light appeared in one of the overhead windows, followed shortly thereafter by another on the floor above. In another few moments the door was opened by the housekeeper, an elderly woman, half asleep, who stood upon the threshold in her nightcap and dressing gown.

"I am extremely sorry to disturb you," the detective informed her briskly, "but it is absolutely essential that I speak with Dr. Agar at once. My name is Sherlock Holmes." He handed her his card.

She gaped at us, her eyes blinking away sleep.

"Just a moment, sir, please. Won't you gentlemen step into the hall?"

We were obliged to stand there while she closed the door and went upon our errand. Sherlock Holmes paced furiously in the confined space of the vestibule, gnawing at his knuckles.

"It is staring us in the face, I know it," he cried in

exasperation, "but I cannot fathom it, cannot for the life of me!"

The inner door of the hall opened and the housekeeper admitted us, somewhat more alert now, and showed us to Dr. Moore Agar's consulting room, where she turned up the gas and closed the door. This time we had not long to wait. Almost at once the doctor himself—tall, spare, and distinguished—swept into the room, tying the belt of his red silk dressing gown but otherwise appearing wide awake.*

"Mr. Holmes, what is the meaning of this? Are you ill?"

"I trust not, doctor. I have come to you in a crisis, however, for a piece of information upon which the lives of many may well depend. Forgive me if I do not take time for introductions, though I suspect you already know Dr. Watson."

"Tell me what you need to know, and I will try to help you," Agar informed him without standing on ceremony. If he was in any way discomfited by the lateness of the hour or perturbed by our unannounced arrival, he gave no outward sign of it.

"Very well. I need the name of the leading specialist in tropical diseases here in London."

"Tropical diseases?" He frowned, passing a graceful hand across his mouth as he considered the request. "Well, Ainstree is the man who—"

"He is not at present in England," I pointed out.

"Ha. No, indeed not." The physician suppressed a yawn that was meant to attribute his lapse of memory to the hour.

"Let me see, then—"

"Every minute is of the utmost urgency, Dr. Agar."

"I understand you, sir." He thought a moment

---

* In *The Adventure of the Devil's Foot* (1897) Watson says that one day he will recount the dramatic first meeting of Holmes and Dr. Agar. This would appear to be it.

longer, his blue eyes unblinking; then suddenly he snapped his fingers. "It comes to me now. There is a young man who might be able to assist you. His name escapes me, but I can look him up in my study and it won't take but a minute. Wait here."

He took a piece of paper from his desk and disappeared from the office. Holmes continued to pace restlessly, like a caged animal.

"Just look at this place," Shaw growled, taking in the plush surroundings with a sweep of his small arm. "Fancy bound books and gadgets galore! The medical profession could easily compete with the theatre as a house of illusion if it wanted to. Does any of this paraphernalia really assist in curing folk of their ailments, or are these all a collection of stage props designed to impress the patient with the majesty and power of the shaman?"

"If the patient is cured by illusion, that is no less a cure," I protested, whereat Shaw regarded me with a curious stare. I confess that once again I was nettled by the fellow's caustic observations, but Holmes, seemingly oblivious to the exchange, continued to pace about the room.

"So," Shaw went on, "if a man contracts the plague and goes to see a physician about it, by your argument, a roomful of books and instruments, such as these——"

"Plague!"

Holmes spun around, his face dead white, his hands shaking. "Plague," he repeated in an almost reverential tone. "That is what we are dealing with."

Never had a single word struck such terror in the very roots of my soul.

"Plague?" I repeated faintly, suppressing a shudder of dread. "How can you know?"

"Watson, invaluable Watson! You held the key in your own hands from the first! Do you remember the line you quoted from Act three, Scene one, of *Romeo and Juliet*?: 'A *plague* on both your houses!' He was being literal! And what did they do when the plague came to London?"

"They closed the playhouses," Shaw interjected.

"Precisely."

At this moment the door opened and Agar returned, a folded piece of paper in his hand.

"I have the name you asked for," he informed the detective, holding forth the paper.

"I know already what name it is," Holmes responded, taking it. "Ah, you have included his address. That is most helpful. Ah, yes, before me all the time, and I was blind to it! Quick, Watson!" He stuffed the paper into the pocket of his Inverness. "Dr. Agar—" he grabbed the astonished physician's hand and pumped it in passing—"a thousand thanks!" He tore from the room, leaving us no alternative but to pursue him.

The cab was waiting for us as ordered, and Holmes leapt in, yelling to the driver, "Thirty-three Wyndham Place, Marylebone, and don't spare the horse!" We had barely time to clamber in after him before the vehicle was tearing through the nocturnal city of London with an echoing clatter of hoofbeats.

"All the time, all the time," was the insistent litany of Sherlock Holmes, intoned again and again as we raced through the deserted streets on our fateful errand. "When you have eliminated the impossible whatever remains, however improbable, must be the truth. If only I had heeded that simple maxim!" he groaned. "Watson, you are in the presence of the greatest fool in Christendom."

"I believe we are in the presence of the greatest lunatic," Shaw broke in. "Pull yourself together, man, and tell us what's afoot."

My companion leaned forward, his grey eyes flashing like lighthouse beacons in the dark.

"The game, my dear Shaw! The game's afoot, and such a quarry as I've never been faced with yet! The greatest game of my career, and should I fail to snare it, we may all very well be doomed!"

"Can you not speak more plainly, in heaven's name? I think I've never heard such melodrama outside of the Haymarket!"

Holmes sat back and looked calmly about him. "You don't need to listen to me at all. In a very few minutes you shall hear it from the lips of the man we are seeking—if he is still alive."

"Still alive?"

"He can't have toyed with the disease as much as he has done without succumbing to it sooner or later."

"Plague?"

Holmes nodded. "Sometime in the mid-fourteenth century three ships carrying spices from the East put into port in Genoa. In addition to their cargo they carried rats, which left the ship and mingled with the city's own rodents. Shortly dead rats began appearing in streets everywhere, thousands of them. And then the human populace began to die. The symptoms were simple: dizziness, headache, sore throat, and then hard black boils under the arms and around the groin. After the boils—fever, shivering, nausea, and spitting blood. In three days the victim was dead. Bubonic plague. In the next fifty years it killed almost half the population of Europe, with a mortality rate of ninety percent of all it infected. People referred to it as the Black Death, and it must easily rank as the greatest natural disaster in human history."

"Where did it come from?" We found ourselves talking in whispers.

"From China, and from thence to India. The Crusaders and then the merchants brought it home with them—it destroyed Europe and then disappeared as suddenly as it erupted."

"And never returned?"

"Not for three hundred years. In the mid-seventeenth century, as Shaw recalled, they were forced to close the playhouses when it reached England. The great fire of London appeared to have ended it then."

"But it's not been heard from since, surely."

"On the contrary, my dear Watson, it has been heard from—and only as recently as last year."

"Where?"

"In China. It erupted with an old vengeance: sprang out of Hong Kong and is at present decimating India, as you know from the papers."

It was difficult, I owned, to associate the bubonic plague that one read of in the newspapers with something as primitively awesome as the Black Death—and even more difficult to envisage another onslaught of the fatal pestilence here in England.

"Nevertheless, we are now facing that possibility," Sherlock Holmes returned. "Ah, here we are. Hurry, gentlemen!" He dismissed the cab and dashed up the steps of number 33, where we discovered the door to be unbolted. Cautiously Holmes pushed it open. Almost at once our nostrils were assailed by the most terrible odor.

"What is it?" Shaw gasped, reeling on the front step.

"Carbolic."

"Carbolic?"

"In enormous concentration. Cover your noses and mouths, gentlemen. Watson, you haven't your revolver with you? No? What a pity. Inside, please." So saying, he plucked forth his own handkerchief and, pressing it to his face, moved into the house.

The lamps were off, and we dared not light the gas for fear of disturbing the occupants, though how anyone should have passed a decent night in that pungent atmosphere, I could not imagine.

Gradually, making our way back along the first

floor, we became aware of a rasping, rhythmic sound, rather like the pulse-beat of some piece of machinery in need of an oil can.

Instinctively we made our way towards that pumping sound and found ourselves in a darkened room.

"Come no nearer!" a voice rasped suddenly, very close by. "Mr. Holmes is it? I have been waiting for you." I was aware of a shrouded figure, slumped in a chair somewhere across the room by the windows which faced the street.

"I hoped we would find you in time, Dr. Benjamin Eccles."

Slowly the figure moved in the dark and, with a groan of effort, managed to turn up the gas.

# FIFTEEN

# Jack Point

It was indeed the theatre doctor who was revealed to us by the faint light of the lone lamp.

But so changed! His body, like that of a wizened old monkey, sat shrunk in its chair, and I should scarcely have recognised the face as human, let alone his, had Holmes not identified him for us. His countenance was withered, like a rotten apple, covered with hideous black boils and pustules that split and poured forth bile like dirty tears. The stuff ran down his bumpy face and made it glisten. His eyes were so puffed and bloodshot that he could hardly open them; the whites, glimpsed beneath the lids, rolled horribly around. His lips were cracked and parched and split, with bleeding sores. With a chill shock shooting through my bones, I realised that the rasping, pump-like sound we had been listening to was his own laboured breath, wheezing like the wind through a pipe organ—and the knowledge told me that Dr. Eccles had not another hour to live.

"Come no closer," the apparition repeated in a husky whisper. "I am going fast and must be left alone until I do. Afterwards you must burn this room and everything in it, especially my corpse—I've written it down here in case you came too late—but whatever you do, do not touch the corpse! Do you understand? Do not touch it!" he croaked. "The disease is transmitted by contact with the flesh!"

"Your instructions shall be carried out to the letter," Holmes answered firmly. "Is there any way we can make you more comfortable?"

The putrescent mass shook slowly from side to side, a black, swollen tongue lolling loosely from what had once been a mouth.

"There is nothing you can do for me—and nothing I deserve. I am dying of my own folly and merit all the pain my wickedness has brought me. But God knows I loved her, Mr. Holmes! As surely as a man ever loved a woman in this world, I loved Jessie Rutland, and no man since time started was ever forced to do for his love what fate made me do for mine!" He gave a choked sob that wracked all that remained of his miserable frame, and it almost carried him off then and there. For a full minute we were obliged to listen to his dreadful sounds, until at length they subsided.

"I am a Catholic," said he, when he could speak again. "For obvious reasons, I cannot send for a priest. Will you hear my confession?"

"We will hear it," my companion answered gently. "Can you speak?"

"I can. I must!" With a superhuman effort the creature hoisted himself straighter in his chair. "I was born not far from here, in Sussex, just over forty years ago. My parents were well-to-do country folk, and though I was a second son, I was my mother's favourite and received an excellent education. I was at Winchester and then at the University of Edinburgh, where I took my medical degree. I passed my examinations with flying colours, and all my professors agreed that my strength lay in research. I was a young man, however, with a head crammed full of adventurous yearnings and ideas. I'd spent so much time studying, I craved a little action before settling down to my test tubes and microscope. I wanted to see a little of life before I immured myself within the cloistered walls of a laboratory, so I enrolled in the course for army surgeons at Netley. I arrived in India in the wake of the mutiny, and for fifteen years I led the life I dreamed of, serving under Braddock and later Fitzpatrick. I saw action in the Second Afghan War and, even like yourself, Dr. Watson, I was at Maiwand. All the time I kept notebooks and recorded the things I found in my travels, mainly observations on tropical disorders I encountered in my capacity as army doctor—for I was determined, eventually, to follow my true calling and take up research."

He stopped here and again broke into a series of heaving coughs, spitting blood upon the carpet. There was some water in a glass and a carafe just out of reach on the table beside him, and Shaw made to move it nearer.

"Back, fool!" he gasped. "Can you not understand?" With an effort of will he seized the glass and greedily gulped down its contents, the water gurgling through his distended intestines, so that all could hear it.

"Five years ago I left the army and settled in Bombay to pursue research at the Hospital for Tropic Diseases there. I had by this time married Edith Morstan, the niece of a captain in my regiment, and we took a house near my work, preparing ourselves for a happy and rewarding future together. I don't know that I loved her the way I came to love Jessie, but I meant to do right by her as a husband and a father, and I did it, too, so far as it was within my power. Up until that time, Mr. Holmes, I was a happy man! Life had smiled upon me from the first, and everything I had touched had turned to gold. As a student, as a

soldier, as a surgeon, and as a suitor my efforts were
always crowned with success." *

He paused, remembering his life, it seemed. Something very like a smile played upon what remained of
his features and then vanished.

"But overnight it all ended. As suddenly and arbi-
trarily as though I'd been allotted a store of good
fortune and used it all up, disaster overtook me. It
happened in this way. Within two years of my marriage, my wife, whose heart condition I had known of
from the first days of our courtship, suffered an attack
that left her little more than a living corpse, unable to
speak, hear, see, or move. It came like a thunderbolt
from the blue. I had seen men die or lose their limbs
in battle, but never before had catastrophe blighted me
or mine. There was nothing for it but to put her in the
nursing home run in conjunction with the hospital—
she who only the day before had been my own dear
girl.

"At first I visited her every day, but seeing that my
visits made no impression on her and only served to
rend my own heart, I reduced their frequency and
finally stopped going altogether, satisfying myself with
weekly reports on her condition, which was always the
same, no better or worse than before. The law pre-
cluded any question of divorce. In any event, I had no
desire to marry again. It was the last thing in my mind
as I continued my work in the hospital laboratory.

"For a time my life took on a new routine, and I
came to assume that I was finished with disaster. But
disaster had only begun with me! My father wrote to
say he was not well, but I hesitated to return home,
fearing to leave my wife. Thus, he died without seeing
me again, and my elder brother succeeded to his estate.

* Eccles's life almost parallels Watson's in many ways, but
in none so astonishing as his wife's maiden name. Could
Edith Morstan have been a cousin to Mrs. Watson?

After my father's demise, my mother wrote, begging me to return, but again I refused, saying that I could not leave Edith—and soon my mother died, herself. I think she died of double grief—my father's death coupled with my refusal to come home.

"And then last year, as if all that had gone before it were but a foolish prelude, a light-hearted glimpse at things to come, there came the plague from China. It tore through India like a veritable scourge of God, sweeping all before it. By the millions people died! Oh, I know you've read it in the papers, but it was quite another thing to be there, gentlemen, I assure you! All the Asian subcontinent turned into one vast charnel house, with only a comparative handful of medical men to sort out the situation and fight it. In all my experience as a physician I had never before beheld the like. It came in two forms: bubonic, transmitted by rats, and pneumonic, which infects the lungs and is transmitted by humans. By virtue of my previous research in the area of infectious diseases, I was one of the first five physicians named to the Plague Board, formed by Her Majesty's government to combat the epidemic. I was put in charge of investigations into the pneumonic variety of plague and set to work at once.

"In the meantime, the plague raced through Bombay itself, killing hundreds of thousands, but my ill luck stayed with me and my wife remained untouched. Do not misunderstand me. I did not wish her to die like this—" he gestured feebly to himself—"but I knew what a burden her life was, and I prayed for her to be stricken and put out of her misery. May God forgive me for that prayer!" he cried fervently.

He paused again, this time for breath, and sat there panting and wheezing like some ghastly bellows. Then, summoning reserves of strength I did not expect remained in him, he leaned forward, seized the carafe, and drank from it, holding it unsteadily to his face and dribbling much water down his chin and on to his open collar. When he had done, he let it fall to the floor, where the carpet prevented its breaking.

"The Plague Board decided to send me to England," he resumed. "Someone had to continue research while others actually fought the disease. I had had some slight luck with a tincture of iodine preparation, provided it was applied within twelve hours of exposure, and the board wished me to experiment with the possibilities of vaccination based upon my formula. It was decided that the work could better be continued in England, as the ravages of the malady itself severely limited facilities and equipment, as well as making it more difficult to ensure absolute control over the experiments.

"This decision was by no means painful to me. On the contrary, it salved my conscience with a real excuse to quit that pestilent place, which contained so many bad memories for me, including a wife I could neither cure nor destroy. For years I had contemplated abandoning my life in India, and now the legitimate opportunity had been afforded me. All due precautions were taken, and I brought samples of pneumonic plague bacillus with me to St. Bartholomew's Hospital here in London, where an emergency laboratory was placed at my disposal. I continued my investigations with a vengeance, studying the plague, its cause and cure, relying heavily on the work of Shibasaburo Kitasato, director of the Imperial Japanese Institute for the Study of Infectious Diseases, and Alexandre Yersin, a bacteriologist in Switzerland. Last year both these men isolated a rod-shaped bacterial micro-organism called *Pasteurella pestis,* vital to the progress of my work.

"I laboured long and hard to integrate their findings with my own but found that when evenings came, I could stand it no longer. My mind was stagnating for lack of recreation or other occupation. I knew virtually no-one in London and did not care to speak with my

brother, so it was hard for me. And then I heard of
the post vacated by Dr. Lewis Spellman, the theatre
physician on call in the West End, who was retiring.
I visited Dr. Spellman and ascertained that the work
was not really difficult and would serve to occupy my
evenings in a pleasant and diverting fashion. I had
never known any theatre people, and I thought the job
would certainly provide me with some human contact,
sadly lacking in my life of late.

"Upon Dr. Spellman's recommendation I was given
the post some months ago, and it made a considerable
difference in my life. The work was scarcely exacting,
and I was seldom called upon to treat more than an
untimely sore throat, though I once had occasion to
set a fractured arm suffered by an actor during a fall
in a duel. All in all, it was a distinct contrast to the
desperate search I was engaged in at Bart's. I would
scrub myself down at the end of every day, using the
tincture of iodine solution, and eagerly proceed upon
my theatrical rounds. When I had finished my tour of
an evening, I returned here to my lodgings, pleasantly
enervated and mentally refreshed.

"It was in this way that I came to meet Jessie Rutland. It had been years since I thought of a woman,
and it was only by degrees that I noticed and became
attracted to her. In our conversations I made no mention of my wife or her condition, as the subject never
came up. Later, when it was relevant, I feared to tell
her of it.

"That was the beginning, gentlemen. All was perfectly correct between us, for we had not acknowledged the depth of our feelings and we were both
aware of the rules governing contact between the sexes
at the Savoy.

"Yet, slowly we came to love each other, Mr.
Holmes. She was the sweetest, most generous creature
under a bonnet, with the most loving and tender dis-

position. I saw in her love the chance for my soul's salvation. It was then that I told her of my marriage. It caused me agony for weeks beforehand, but I decided I had no right to keep the facts from someone I loved so dearly and so made a clean breast of it."

He stopped to catch his breath, the whites of his eyes winking madly at us, rolling about in their sockets.

"She was very distraught at first, and I thought my worst fears were confirmed. For three days she refused to speak to me, and during that time I thought I must become lunatic. I was ready to do away with myself when she relented and told me that she loved me still. I cannot tell you into what transports of joy that knowledge put me. I felt there were no obstacles that could not be overcome, nothing I could not accomplish with her at my side and her love in my heart!

"But Fate had not yet done with me. Just as it had done in the past, it struck not at me directly but through the woman I loved. A man—an ogre, I should say—approached Jessie without my knowing of it and told her he knew of our intrigue. He had made enquiries of his own and said he knew I was married. He twisted our love into something sordid and terrifying. His whispers were without shame and without remorse—and she succumbed to them. She acted partly for my sake, as well as for her own, in submitting to his lecherous fancy, for he had played upon her fears in that respect, and she told me nothing of what she had done, lest she compromise us both and add my ruin to her own.

"But she couldn't keep secret her emotions, Mr. Holmes. That intuitive bond that exists between two people in love had already sprung up between us and without knowing what had happened, I knew something was wrong. With many sighs and tears I pried the tale of her humiliation from her, promising beforehand that whatever I heard, I would take no action.

"But it was no use my making such a promise! What she told me was too monstrous to be believed, let alone endured. There was something so incredible about such casual, yet total malevolence that I had to see it for myself.

"I went to his house and spoke with him—" he paused, coughing slightly and shaking his head. "I had never met such a man in all my travels. When I confronted him with his shameful deed, he laughed! Yes, laughed to hear me throw it to his face and said I didn't know much about the ways of the theatre! I was so taken aback by the colossal effrontery of the thing that I found myself pleading with him—yes, *begging* him—to return to me my life, my world. And still he laughed and patted me jovially on the shoulder, saying I was a good fellow but warning me to stay clear of actresses, as he escorted me to the door of his flat!

"For the entire night I walked the streets of London, venturing into places I didn't know then and couldn't name now as I forced myself to digest my own damnation. During that interminable odyssey something snapped in my mind and I became mad. It was as though all my ill luck had resolved itself into one crystalline shape and that shape belonged to Jonathan McCarthy. On his shoulders I heaped my catalogue of misfortune and travail—my wife's illness, my parents' deaths, the plague itself, and finally, that for which he was truly responsible, the debauch of the woman I loved. She, who was all in the world that was left to me. To picture her in the arms of that bearded Lucifer was more than flesh and blood could bear, and a horrible thought came to me in the early hours of that morning as I stumbled about the city. It had all the perverse logic of the truly insane. If Jonathan McCarthy were Lucifer, why should not I let him wrestle with the scourge of God? I chuckled madly at the notion. Gone were thoughts of science, responsibility, my work; the implications of my fantasies, even, did not exist. All my sinews were bent upon vengeance— horrible and terrible retribution that knew neither reason nor restraint.

"It scarcely matters how I did it; what matters is that I exposed Jonathan McCarthy to pneumonic plague. I know how you are looking at me now; I know full well what you must think of me, gentlemen —and in fact, as the hours ticked by afterwards, I came to share your opinion of the deed. No man was worthy of such a death. Having come to my senses, it was now borne in upon me with a rush—the full impact of what I had done. The terrible forces I had unleashed must be contained before they could wreak havoc on a scale unknown in modern times. All England, possibly all of Western Europe, had been threatened by my folly.

"My conversion to sanity lasted roughly twelve hours. At the end of that time I rushed to McCarthy's flat to warn him of his danger and do what I could for him—but he was not there. In vain I searched all London for the man, stopping at the theatres and restaurants I knew were frequented by members of the literary profession. No-one had seen him. I left a message at his flat finally, and he sent word that he would see me that night. I had no choice but to wait for him while every hour took him further and further from my power to save him and increased the danger to the world. My tincture of iodine solution I had now perfected for induction by mouth, but it still depended on being administered within the first twelve hours.

"I found him at home that evening, as he had promised, and in halting but urgent sentences, I told him what I had done."

Eccles began to cough again and spat great quantities of blood as we watched, our handkerchiefs still pressed to our mouths and noses to avoid the stench of carbolic and putrefaction, our minds numb with horror. He fell back in his chair, exhausted, when he had done, his breath coming more painfully now with every inhalation. Were it not for the noise he made breathing, we should have thought him dead.

When next he spoke, his words were slurred as though he could not form them with the muscles remaining at his disposal: "He laughed at me *again!* Oh, he knew what my real work was, but he didn't think me capable of such an action. Jack Point, he called me and laughed when I tried to make him swallow my tincture of iodine solution with a little brandy. 'If I am infected,' he chuckled, 'you must be sure and call upon Miss Rutland with your potion. She'll be in a worse way by far!' He laughed again, long and hard this time, until I knew and understood why I had been unable to find him for the past twelve hours. And when I *did* comprehend, comprehend that my actions and his had doomed all three of us—and perhaps millions, besides!—I seized a letter opener from his desk and stabbed him with it."

He sighed with a noise like kettledrums, and I knew the sands of his clock were running quickly out.

"From then on, events unfolded with the inevitable precision of a machine built to destroy itself. Jessie was doomed. My antidote would have no effect by the time I reached her. The only question was whether I could prevent her suffering. I waited for her in her dressing room and sent her to heaven when she walked into my arms. I did it as mercifully as I could—" real tears were rolling down his cheeks, now in addition to the pus—"and then I walked 'round to the front of the theatre and entered as though on my evening tour. Stunned, as though that were the truth, I performed an autopsy on the woman I had just slain, while the bloodstained scalpel nestled in my bag under all your noses."

He covered his face with swollen black hands that now resembled claws, and he seemed unable to continue, overcome not only by the ravages of his disease but by his own emotions.

Sensing this, Sherlock Holmes spoke quietly: "If you find it difficult to talk, Doctor, perhaps you will allow me to take up the story as I understand it. You have only to say 'Yes' or 'No' or merely shake your head if you prefer. Is that agreeable to you?"

"Yes."

"Very well." Holmes spoke slowly and distinctly so that he might hear and understand every word before responding: "When you came through the theatre to perform your autopsy, you discovered Dr. Watson and myself already at the dressing room, exposing ourselves to contamination. From our presence there, you could not but infer that we were already involved with the case."

"Yes."

"Mr. Gilbert and Mr. D'Oyly Carte stayed outside the dressing room during our examination; hence, they ran no risk, but Watson and I, as well as you, were now in danger. You heard me say we were going to Simpson's, and you followed us there, waiting for us outside with your antidote."

"Yes."

"While watching us through the window, you perceived that we were joined by a third gentleman—" he gestured to Shaw but Eccles, his eyes closed now, could not see him—"and, wishing to take no chances, you gave him the antidote to drink, as well, as we left the restaurant, happily one by one, which simplified your task."

"Yes. I didn't wish to kill anybody."

"Anybody else, you mean," the detective amended sternly.

"Yes."

"Then you sent a note, warning us out of the Strand."

"I didn't know how else to stop you," Eccles gasped, struggling to open his eyes and face his confessor. "There was nothing for it but to threaten. I would never have done anything."

"As long as we didn't expose ourselves to the plague. For those, like Brownlow, who did, you had no choice."

"No choice: His job killed him, for I knew he must discover my secret. Having been a doctor in the army, I knew that only the coroner would have direct contact with the corpse of a murdered man, and I counted on him to deal with his assistants and stretcher-bearers. Certainly, I could never have managed to deal with them all. But he settled my mind on that score. And we scrubbed down the lab together."

"Then you left together?"

He nodded, his head moving like a drugged man. "I knew when he recognised the symptoms he would dismiss the others and make them scrub. That left only him. My time was limited now, as well. I had already begun to turn into this." He gestured feebly with a talon to himself. "I went 'round to the back of the laboratory and spoke to him through the door, telling him that I knew of his predicament and could help him."

"You helped him to his maker."

Eccles did not move but sat like a grotesque statue of mouldy clay. Suddenly, he began to sob and choke and scream all at once, struggling to rise from his chair and clutching wildly at his abdomen.

"Oh, God have mercy on their souls!" He opened his mouth again, wanting to say more, but sank slowly to the floor in a crumpled heap. There was silence in the room as the light of dawn began to filter through the curtains, as though to dispel the end of a nightmare.

"He prayed for *them*," Shaw murmured, the handkerchief still pressed to his face. "The human race surprises me sometimes in a way that confounds my philosophy." He spoke in an unsteady voice and leaned against the door frame, as though about to faint.

"*In nomine Patris et Filii et Spiritu Sancti*," said Sherlock Holmes, drawing the sign of the Cross in the foetid air. "Has anyone a match?"

And so it was that in the early morning hours of March 3, 1895, a fire broke out at 33 Wyndham Place, Marylebone, and mingled with the rosy red and gold-tongued flames of dawn. By the time the fire brigades reached the spot, the house was almost consumed, and the body of the lone occupant was found burned beyond all possible recognition or preservation. Sherlock Holmes had poured kerosene over it before we walked out of the door and into the new day.

# Epilogue

Achmet Singh walked across the narrow confines of his cell towards Sherlock Holmes and peered at him from behind his thick spectacles.

"They tell me I am free."

"And so you are."

"You have done this?"

"The truth has set you free, Achmet Singh. There is some concern for it yet in this reeling world."

"And Miss Rutland's killer?"

"God has punished him more harshly than any jury would have done."

"I see." The Parsee hesitated, indecisive, and then, with a mighty sob, fell upon his knees, seized the detective's hand, and kissed it.

"You—Sherlock Holmes—breaker of my shackles —from my heart's depths I thank you!"

Indeed, he had much for which to be grateful, though he would never know *how* much. Securing his release from prison and having the charges against him dropped was one of the more difficult feats of Sherlock Holmes's long and surprising career. He was obliged to make Inspector Lestrade appear ridiculous in public—something he was at pains never to

do—and he did it with the full knowledge and coopera-
tion of the inspector, first swearing him to secrecy
and then divulging the entire truth behind the closed
doors of the latter's office. They sat closeted together
for over an hour while the detective explained the implications of what had happened and the need to prevent the truth from becoming generally known, lest
the panic which would inevitably follow prove worse
than the plague itself. The detective managed to suppress all reference to Sergeant Hopkins's nocturnal
initiative, and the inspector, preoccupied with the meat
of the case, never thought to ask how Holmes had
learned of Mr. Brownlow's disappearance with the
corpses before knowledge of it was made public.

In addition, we spent an anxious week waiting to
see if Benjamin Eccles had accomplished his mission
and truly managed to murder everyone who had contracted pneumonic plague and to dispose of their
bodies. There was some question as to the health of
the Savoy chorus, and both Gilbert and D'Oyly Carte
were ordered intensive medical examinations, which,
happily, failed to reveal a trace of the disease.

Bernard Shaw, as most people know, continued
working as a critic but remained true to his promise
and kept writing plays until they made him wealthy
and famous. His curious attitude towards social reform
and personal wealth persisted as long as we knew him.
He and the detective remained eccentric friends to the
last. They saw one another less as Shaw grew more in
demand, but they maintained a lively correspondence,
some of which is in my possession and which includes
the following exchange of telegrams:

TO SHERLOCK HOLMES:
    ENCLOSED PLEASE FIND TWO TICKETS TO OPEN-
    ING NIGHT OF MY NEW PLAY, *Pygmalion*. BRING
    FRIEND IF YOU HAVE ONE.

                                    G. B. S.

TO BERNARD SHAW:

> UNABLE TO ATTEND OPENING NIGHT OF *Pygmalion*. WILL ATTEND SECOND NIGHT IF YOU HAVE ONE.

> HOLMES *

Holmes and I returned to Baker Street later that day, feeling as though we'd just come back from the moon, so long had we been gone and so singular had been our experiences while away. The last few days seemed like aeons.

For a day or so we sat around our rooms like automatons, unable, I think, to fully digest the terrible events in which we had taken part. And then, bit by bit, we fell into our old ways. Another storm blew silently outside our windows, and Holmes found himself again immersed in his chemical experiments. Finally his notes on ancient English charters were once more in his hands.

It was a month later when he threw down the paper at breakfast one morning and looked at me across the table. "We must definitely go to Cambridge, Watson, or I shall not accomplish anything constructive with my research.† How does tomorrow strike you?"

He stalked into his bedroom, leaving me to the

---

\* For years this exchange was erroneously attributed to Shaw and Winston Churchill.

† For details of Holmes's Cambridge experience the reader is urged to consult the case labeled by Watson *The Adventure of the Three Students*. According to Baring-Gould's chronology, this case began on April 5, 1895, almost immediately after the news about Wilde appeared in the papers. This significant jibing of dates goes a long way—in my opinion—towards certifying the authenticity of *The West End Horror*, added to which fact, Holmes's work in Cambridge is not generally conceded to be his best, which also makes sense if we consider that he was operating under something of an emotional strain.

coffee and paper, where I discovered his motive for leaving town so abruptly.

Speculation was rife that Oscar Wilde would shortly be charged with offences under the Criminal Law Amendment Act of 1885.† The subject of Wilde brought back memories of our adventure the previous month.

I followed Holmes into his room, the paper in my hand and on my lips a question that had never occurred to me. "Holmes, there is something that puzzles me about Dr. Benjamin Eccles."

"A great deal, I shouldn't wonder. He was a complicated individual. As I have said before, Watson, a doctor is the first of criminals. He has brains, and he has knowledge; should he care to pervert either, there is a great potential for mischief. Will you hand me that brown tie? Thank you."

"Why, then, did he allow himself to die?" I asked. "Had he taken his own antidote with the zeal he pressed it on others, he might have survived."

My companion paused before replying, taking a coal from the fire and lighting his pipe with it. "We shall probably never know the truth. It may be that he had taken the potion before and in so doing had exhausted its curative properties. Or it may be that he had no wish to live. Some people are not only murderers but judges, juries, and their own executioners, as well, and in those capacities they mete out punishments far more severe than their fellow creatures could devise." He rose from a bootlace. "Do you think it too early in the day for a glass of sherry and a biscuit?"

† Wilde was charged on April 6, 1895. His first trial ended in a hung jury on May 1. On May 20 a second trial was held, and on May 25, 1895, Wilde was found guilty and sentenced to two years' imprisonment with hard labor.

# Acknowledgements

It is again time to pay off a happy debt and thank a number of people for their help, inspiration, encouragement, and critical acumen in preparing the manuscript of *The West End Horror*.

First and foremost, this book could not have been thought of but for the genius of Sir Arthur Conan Doyle. Without his immortal creations, Sherlock Holmes and Dr. Watson, nothing in the way of this story could have been written. It is a tribute to the enormous popularity of Doyle's characters that people are interested in reading stories about them even though their creator is not around to keep supplying them.

After Doyle, I must acknowledge the help and inspiration I found in the works of W. S. Baring-Gould, whose Holmesian chronology I freely accept and whose theories I continue to find charming and provocative.

Probably the foremost living authority on Sherlock Holmes and his world is Mr. Michael Harrison, whose books on the subject I have pored over to advantage, and whom I had the great privilege of meeting. In addition to the use of his books, Mr. Harrison generously allowed me to pick his brain by offering to inspect the manuscript itself and tell me when I was going either astray or too far, two predilections of mine. He made innumerable comments and suggestions, all of great assistance in achieving literary and historical authenticity, and most of which I adopted without hesitation. Where my book remains inaccurate, the blame must fall not upon Mr. Harrison but on my own stubborn insistence on some point or other. Also, I am indebted to Mr. Michael Holroyd for drawing my attention to several crucial questions in the text.

After these four gentlemen, a host of friends and critics crowd the list, some of them Sherlockian enthusiasts, others merely literate. In no particular order I extend my thanks to Craig Fisher, Michael and Constance Pressman, Bob Bookman, Leni Kreitman, Brooke Hopper, Ulu Grossbard, Michael Scheff, Jon Brauer, and Miss Julie Leff, who put up with a great deal of nonsense. My father, of course, has put up with it much longer, and he deserves thanks here, too.

In addition to those who provided literary assistance, I wish to thank Herb Ross, my collaborator on the film version of *The Seven-Per-Cent Solution*, who managed to keep my interest in things Holmesian alive for many months longer than I thought possible; my lawyers, Tom Pollock, Andy Rigrod, and Jake Bloom, whose contributions to the book are not to be underestimated; and my editor, Juris Jurjevics, who is such a good audience.